Blood Rites
of the Bourgeoisie

Blood Rites of the Bourgeoisie

Stewart Home

Semina No. 7

After Death: The Artist

1. Make Kara Walker Tremble with Desire for your Huge New Penis!

It occurs to you that there has been an abstract movement in art but not in fiction. You are interested in how the stratification of the arts might be overcome and decide to inaugurate the first ever exhibition of Abstract Literature. Since Abstract Literature doesn't exist you attempt to conjure it up by producing a definition of it.

'Abstract Literature implodes in a subdued fashion, like a slow motion reversal of an explosion or some other catastrophe. It absorbs all the energy generated by writing as a cultural practice and neutralises it. Abstract Literature is a billowing series of syllables followed by an eruption of colour. It is usually red with purple flashes...'

You know very little about the philosophical sources from which aesthetic theory was constructed. Instead you approach most topics from the perspective of Freud and diagnosis. You decide that Abstract Literature is a product of the subconscious and therefore can't be precisely defined...You don't know that you are already falling behind positions articulated nearly a hundred years ago by the Surrealists.

You imagine the Abstract Literature Manifesto you are attempting to write being played in the key of G major, and you attempt to visualise it as deep space; black with flashes of darker blackness. Your text is pornographic, its obscenity lies in the fact that it can't be imagined, it can only be experienced in its totality as concrete form. Blackness. The void. Too many light-years between stars.

You try to think yourself into a state of suspended animation. You worship waste and claim to be drawing on Bataille's theory of solar economics. If nature abhors a vacuum then nature itself must be a social construction, there is nothing at all in deep space. You want to add some colour to your text...Space is deep.

'An exhausted sun compacted into itself. The slow but painless death of literature... Syllables should be moved around the page like clouds passing across the moon. Dense thickets of rhetoric must grow inexorably into an impenetrable jungle of words that overrun any and all attempts to extract a coherent meaning from them.'

You've ended up mirroring the slow drift of an ice floe, the imperceptible passage of distant galaxies through hyper-space. At this point your words in their opaque nothingness literally become 'the ill-will of the people', the spongy referent that animates all post-democratic societies. The cold of interstellar space thousands of degrees below freezing. Abstract Literature: A New Movement in the Visual Arts!

Non-Euclidean geometries. Voices green, purple and red. Strange folds in the fabric of time and space. The universe buckled, bent and sent into reverse. Apocalypse postponed, time running backwards and in slow-mo. Your words have developed an intolerance to alcohol. They are overwhelmed by feelings of existential dread and can't bear to be separated from each other. They've arranged themselves into a single extended sentence from some eldritch dimension unknown to man, a slow stuttering echo of Molly Bloom's soliloquy at the end of *Ulysses*.

2. At Last, Sexual Satisfaction for Cosey Fanni Tutti with your Bigger and Better Cock!

You have received an exhibition proposal from the Suicide Kid. You don't like it but there is an experimental space in the Museum of Modern Art (London) that doubles as a unisex toilet, where you might do a show of the type she is proposing. MoMA's public funding could be jeopardised if you don't redress your bias towards painting by dead white males. The Suicide Kid ticks various boxes that need to be filled.

The Suicide Kid is a charming transexual foot fetishist and might be described as Paco Ignacio Taibo meets Paracelsus at an Illegal Rave. You wonder whether she has a boyfriend or a girlfriend. You hope she has a girlfriend who can be convinced that you are much more of a 'real' man than the Suicide Kid. You don't have a girlfriend of your own, although you'd like to get married. You see curators as invisible men correcting the faults of others.

You compose an email to the Suicide Kid in which you insist on a minor alteration to the title of the proposed show. You explain that *Lederhosen Kamikaze Death Squat!* will mean nothing to the average MoMA visitor and that if Joe Public and his wife Edna are to engage with the new discipline of Abstract Literature, then a snappier title is required. The 't' at the end of the title must go, and you want to replace it with a 'd'.

While you accept that an artist has the right to deploy a software programme to randomly generate the title of their exhibition, you also believe that good sense dictates the use of verbal intelligibility in these matters. After all, if MoMA didn't entice arses to walk through its doors, then its multi-billion pound public funding might end up being diverted into elitist opera houses or used to subsidise mortgages for first-time buyers.

You try to ignore the fact that one small part of your brain is wondering what it would be like to have sex with a chick with a dick. You are a cultured man not much given to base thoughts. You Google the Suicide Kid and end up on her MySpace profile. You look through her pictures and decide she is hot, although you know she could never replace seventies performance artist Cosey Fanni Tutti as the great unfulfilled love of your life. You spend a long time looking at a set of photographs of the Suicide Kid sunbathing on an Italian beach; you find the bulge in her bikini bottoms particularly arresting.

You feel that somebody needs to take the Suicide Kid in hand, for her own good of course! You know you're the ideal candidate to pull down her skimpy bikini and smack that hot little bottom. You've heard that many transsexuals fund their sex change operations through prostitution, and you wonder if the Suicide Kid does much street walking. You'd certainly like to meet her in a dark alley...

Your thoughts are wandering, and although you know MoMA would never allow you to stage it, you are fantasising about organising an exhibition entitled *Whores On All Fours*. This would feature documentary photographs of transsexual prostitutes getting down on their hands and knees so that they might take a huge schlong up the ass. The visual styling of this show would be based on forensic materials.

3. Split Martha Rosler's Pussy Wide Open with your New Bigger Schlong!

You think of dying planets sucked into long dead stars, black dwarfs, white dwarfs, and entropy. You cannot put these thoughts into words, the meaning slips from you like a ship leaving the docks at Tilbury. Make Iwona Blazwick buckle and moan all night when you split her pussy wide open. The web is absorbing all the energy consumer society has generated over the years and is neutralising it.

You understand very little of the scientific theory underpinning texts on the chemical structure of DNA, and so you read up on the subject because your inability to comprehend it satisfies your lust for abstraction; but this is a pursuit with diminishing returns, since as you read your understanding grows. Mail Scanner has detected a possible fraud attempt! King style for Dorothea, enormous phallus for Eva, king-size cock for Dorothea!

In Abstract Literature words come across like a sixties Art Happening, all jumbled and confused. Viagra at $1.41 per dose! Best online drug store! Our purpose is to provide PC and Macintosh software and computer solutions at low prices. 'Jacques wuz 'ere 13 October 1307', 'Death Lives, Oedipus Wrecks!', 'Jacques de Molay thou art avenged!', 'Never Work!'

You call down a search engine and check Time Server out online. He has a Facebook account, but isn't on MySpace or Flickr. You wonder how he survives in London on a MoMA assistant curator's wage, which you estimate as being possibly 20K a year; but then you survive in London on even lower freelance earnings than that. Our safe, secure games will get you smiling. Download our casino in twenty seconds to get $999 richer when you join. Relax and have fun with poker, blackjack, roulette and progressive video slots!

You feel a certain amount of sympathy for the Time Server, since you understand that under capitalism we all reproduce our own alienation, but he has nonetheless become your target. This isn't a shoot 'em up game—you're gonna burn the bastard, show him how fresh and bad you are. Theatre is dead. Cinema is dead. Literature is dead. Time and space died yesterday. You eat dead food, you fuck dead men, even your words die in your mouth. Your sentences are rolled into the ebbing waters of modernism and then wash back like a bulimic's forced vomiting.

Get your free $2,400 again and again. We draw your attention to the new messages in your private box. $2,400 welcome bonus will be deposited in your new casino account! We pay you to play. Top quality luxury watches offered at discount prices!! Travel no further than your screen and get your free $2,400! Click to buy Viagra for as low as $1.53. Even if you have no erection problems! How about the best service around? Best offer in gambling history! Win $$$ instead of throwing it all away at other casinos. Get $2,400 when you download our casino. Remember we always SHIP things free of cost. We have all kinds of BIG brand shoes for you to purchase online. Just one click away from you! 100% genuine quality and discounted price! Gucci, Prada, D&G, Versace, Chanel, Ugg. Enlarge your penis at no extra cost!

4. Sam Taylor (Gives You) Wood...

You open an email from the Suicide Kid, it doesn't make much sense, but that is irrelevant. His skills are visual not verbal. He is lucky to be dealing with you as a curator, since you can interpret what he is saying and make it accessible to the public. You are in fact an assistant curator, and you know you deserve promotion to a top job, although you've been damned with a subtitle for the past dozen years. You open an attachment from the Suicide Kid that makes even less sense than his email.

Zero. One. Zero.

You don't understand computer art. You're not impressed by the tagging and graffiti the Suicide Kid did as a teenager either. You still believe the White Cube is a sanctified space and you're glad the former street artist you are dealing with has been moving in that direction. For some reason your inbox is being flooded with spam messages.

Enlarge your penis with our magic pills! It's as easy as one, two, three! You won't have to worry about the size anymore. Link to Elizabeth McAlpine's private pictures (link missing). You look so familiar! Have we met? Hey, what's up? I believe we got drunk together at a party last week. Are you the guy that took Elizabeth home? Elizabeth told me she had a wonderful time with you! Anyway Elizabeth just gets sexier and sexier. Here's the link to Elizabeth's private pictures, PLEASE do not give this out to anyone, this is for you ONLY! Check out her private pictures NOW!

Mixed with this spam are a growing number of angry messages from highly prestigious international cultural institutions. Most boil down to brusque demands for an explanation as to why emails apparently sent from your computer contain messages of the following type: 'Make Louise Bourgeois buckle and moan all night when you split her pussy wide open.'

So, are you still ready to have a little fun and finally meet? I've been a bit naughty the last couple weeks. I guess I can tell you about it later. Remember my handle: just go here (link missing). Mail Scanner has detected a possible fraud attempt! This is subject to availability. She moans louder now I have gained 3 full inches! Free shipping on all designer footwear from Chanel, Gucci, Prada, Dior, Ugg. Finally the 2012 collections are in, enjoy 70% OFF brand name shoes & boots for men & women from TOP fashion designers. Choose from a variety of the season's hottest models from Gucci, Prada, Chanel, Dior, Ugg, Burberry, D&G, Dsquared² & many more. VISIT now! Save TODAY! Free international shipping on ALL ORDERS! She moans louder and loves sex so much more now that I have gained 3 full inches! Users will be deleted if they don't forward this. Your dick is like a broken vending machine…How are you?

5. Big Strong Erections for Victoria Gold!

You have infected Time Server's computer with the ArtWhore virus, which is now spamming his email contacts with randomly generated obscene messages about famous female artists. The virus also forwards copies of the mail going in and out of the Time Server's mailbox to you, so you have full documentation of the prank.

Hey, I read your profile online a few minutes ago and you seem interesting. Universal compassion is the quality that defines art. Don't set aside the rare attraction of being freed from all sins. Feeling that your dick is working like a broken vending machine? Wait no longer and implement the following instructions (link missing). Spend! Spend! Spend! Satisfied with your penis size? Yes it gets big, yes it gets strong, yes you can do it (link missing). Make Rachel Whiteread's pussy wail like the proverbial cat that got the cream!

As an art prank you plan to disrupt a performance scheduled to take place in Hoxton Square. The work is a re-enactment of a police forensics search for human body parts. You will make fake human body parts from butchers' offal and old bones, then scatter these remains around the park shortly before the performance is scheduled to begin. You will ask passers-by whether they think the remains are animal or human. One of those you approach will pull out their mobile and call the police. The re-enactment will be cancelled and replaced by its double, a 'genuine' forensic examination of the area. You will film as much of the action as you can, since this prank won't be art if you don't document it.

Darkness, light, darkness, light, darkness, light, darkness, light, darkness, light, darkness, light, darkness, light, darkness, light, darkness, light, darkness, light, darkness, light, darkness, light, darkness, light, darkness, light, darkness, light.

You attend a screening of *Trans-Europ-Express* at the British Film Institute. You wonder whether the shaky handheld camera work at the beginning is a homage to, or pastiche of, trends in French cinema that were already moribund by the time Alain Robbe-Grillet directed this film in 1966. As you watch the film you experience a painful flashback to a previous life: you were born in 1962 and saw *Trans-Europ-Express* several times at the Scala Cinema, both in Tottenham Street and after its move to Kings X. In this previous existence you hanged yourself as a work of performance art and donated your body to science.

BTW: did you know that literature is a Nigerian money scam? On the one hand you go to those poetry sites where people cut and paste words and phrases together to form post-modern nonsense then, on the other hand, you get all this spam coming through which uses exactly the same technique to fill out the body of the email and avoid the spam filters while sticking in an image which is an ad for some Venezuelan gerbil-farm's stock offering. It's great. You can't get enough spam which is why you should spend all day submitting your name to as many goofball spam sites as you can. This morning you could have received 230,000 new emails and all of them full of great avant-garde, erm, poetry. Long Live Art!

6. Your Bigger Package Will Satisfy Tom of Finland No End!

Dear Time Server

I have a business proposal. My name is Tony Oursler, you may have heard of my work as a video artist, but I'm also a medical doctor here in New York City. I have a widow in my clinic called Alice B. Topless who is a political refugee in my country. She has been so ill in recent months that I don't expect her to live much longer. Recently Alice Topless revealed to me that she inherited a fortune from her late husband, who as a senior military officer in Sierra Leone (West Africa) bravely met his death by single-handedly delaying for more than three days the storming of a government radio station by thousands of rebels during the civil war. Hundreds of rebels were killed by General Topless in this heroic defence of a democratic regime.

My medical position necessitates quarterly audits of my accounts and I don't have time to take on the functions of an accountant and art consultant. Therefore, this rich widow has asked me to source a credible and trustworthy partner who will manage funds for her young children by investing in cutting edge contemporary art. There is in total a sum of twenty-eight million United States dollars, which her late husband deposited with a fiduciary agent in South Africa.

I believe you are in a position to assist not only in managing this large sum of money but investing it in top of the range contemporary art. Mrs Topless would also need you to help create a safe haven for her children by making a residence arrangement for them in your country. After Alice Topless disclosed this information, I asked her to show me the documents relating to her late husband's twenty-eight million dollars deposit. I now have the legal papers covering the deposit which I can fax as soon as you confirm via email that for a ten per cent cut of all monies involved, you are prepared to help this lady and her children.

Alice B. Topless has only limited knowledge of the business and art worlds, and even if she was well could not manage the funds herself; besides she needs to keep a low profile to avoid rebel government attempts to assassinate her and her children. To proceed I need from you a signed letter of understanding and once I have this we can place the funds into a secure account in your name; this will necessitate you meeting with the fiduciary company agent in Europe to arrange delivery of the deposit via a diplomatic courier system. The funds are sealed in two large trunks that are registered as containing family treasures, so the security company and its agents are unaware of the monetary content of the boxes.

Let me assure you that this transaction is 100% risk free. Since I am sure you know how to invest wisely in contemporary art, for very little effort you could make yourself millions of dollars. All I need is a quick indication of interest from you. Email me at: tonyoursler_law@yahoo.com. Thanks and may God bless you.

Sincere regards, Tony Oursler, medical doctor and video artist.

7. Your Huge Cock Will Make Cindy Sherman Buckle and Moan All Night!

During yet another pointless meeting with the Time Server to discuss your *Abstract Literature* exhibition, the sympathy you once felt for this loser evaporates. He wants you to explain to him how Abstract Literature could be configured in relation to notions such as that of 'the altermodern'. You hate the theoretical duplicities of Nicolas Boring Ass. Boring Ass might have pulled the wool over the eyes of the odd London arts world liberal but he can't fool you. He's an incompetent theorist but he knows what he wants and that's to be the cultural commissar of France. What Boring Ass has to say about 'the altermodern' chimes with the pathetic rhetoric about defending diversity and 'opposing' globalism favoured by the New Right. Boring Ass may claim to be 'post-political' but since he pitches 'the altermodern' as a celebration of 'difference', once his rhetoric is taken outside the gallery it all too easily translates into 'France for the French' and 'England for the English'. You say shit on that for a game of soldiers!

As our dearest client you can be the first to try our new internet page! Only original high-quality drugs at a price hard to beat!! 20% guaranteed abatement for you only!!! Can you imagine that you are healthy? Come to our site & obtain pharmaceuticals sent straight to your home. Are you looking for the cheapest software? We have the software you want dirt cheap. Check for yourself and enjoy all the software you desire for the lowest prices ever!

You're tired of Time Server's rants about the mission of the curator to illuminate a secular world with the light of art...It comes across as a tired re-hash of John Ruskin's *Seven Lamps of Architecture*—superannuated bullshit about the moral value of culture. That said, if Ruskin died a virgin, that was because having devoted too long to studying classical culture, he was so shocked when he discovered real women had pubic hair that it put him off sex for life (but only, of course, if you don't buy the rival theory that he was a serial child abuser). Bringing this up to date, the Time Server simply can't get laid, regardless of whether he tries it on with shaven ravers, air-strips or girls with a full bush.

You check your laptop when Time Server goes to buy more coffee, savouring the cream of new poetry from your inbox. After only two weeks you will notice an amazing difference in girth. You may require a dosage adjustment of Sildenafil or special monitoring during treatment if you are taking other drugs. Viagra at $1.41 per dose! Best online drug store! Prestige and luxury replica watches. Over 8,000 styles of genuine Swiss replica watch. Our purpose is to provide PC and Macintosh software and computer solutions at the lowest possible prices. Whether you're a corporate client, running a small enterprise, or shopping for your home PC, we can help you!

You ask Time Server a simple question and he can't answer it...What is a curator? Originally a curator was someone who looked after what were often religious objects; the word comes from the same Latin root that gives us the Protestant office of curate. But what is a curator in a secular world, and can you curate a magazine or a music festival?...You think not but that doesn't stop other people, including the Time Server, using the phrase in this loose fashion.

8. Give Hanna Wilke the Time of her Life!

You recently gave a lecture, *How the Institution of Art Saved High Culture from the Curse of Post-Modern Kitsch* at the prestigious Republican College of Art in Kensington Gore. After the talk a female student called Karen Eliot spoke with you and said she wanted to do a photo shoot at MoMA. Eliot was pretty and you agreed to help her. Now she is standing naked and with her legs spread wide apart over a table in the MoMA restaurant. You came into work early to help her with this project and as the set up for the shoot progresses you become increasingly nervous. The photographer is placed so that an instantly recognisable London cityscape forms the background to Karen Eliot's naked form. Restaurant staff will begin arriving very soon and you pray none of them turn up early enough to clock Karen Eliot's antics.

Do a rocking hot pair of teenage twins tonight! Used G-strings for sale. Click now for great deals. Stealthily, you grope her from behind, tear away her skirt, then...Wham! Bam! Thank you Mam! Cheap and easy herbal formula adds length. Treat yourself to a size upgrade today. Leading the enhancement revolution! Ancient herbal recipes available now! Your love tool is set to grow. Why wait when you can upsize today? Bring your desire back with herbal infusions! Revolutionary new medical discoveries have made growth of 3 to 6 inches possible.

Why are you still shy? Reinvigorate your sex life by enlarging your tool! Use whatever works!

Karen Eliot, a blond postgraduate, told you she was involved in an art movement called 'female anarchy'. When she urinates all over the restaurant table she's perched upon and the photographer she's brought with her snaps away, you finally recall what you'd heard about 'female anarchy'; adherents document themselves pissing in public places. The resulting photo books have been big sellers in sex shops around the world. You can't believe that you'd forgotten this vital piece of information when you'd agreed to help Karen Eliot, who'd not mentioned urination when she'd asked you to assist by providing a location for a shoot. You realise that if the MoMA management find out about this then you're in danger of losing your job.

Now you can enhance your sex life at the lowest prices. Special suggestions for assistant curators. Save 87% on your pharmaceuticals. A wide range of products sent to your home in a plain brown wrapper. No medical prescriptions required. Fast shipment. Your Coupon TcSBI. Visit us! The secret of pulling the coolest cutie. US $69.95 Viagra 100mg x 10 pills price. US $159.95 price for 100mg x 90 pills. Make her mind up for her. Using this solution you will gain a full 3 inches and instantly boost your confidence. Take 2 tablets a day for massive gains in just a few weeks.

Karen is pleased with the results of her photo shoot. She shows you a picture that makes it look like she's pissing on the London skyline...She reassures you no one will guess it was taken in the MoMA restaurant. She gives you a photo book in which she's shown putting petrol into her car at various European filling stations wearing nothing more than a smile and a pair of high-heeled shoes. Eliot's photographic assistant is mopping up her urine and scrubbing the table down with anti-septic fluid. Your hectic schedule means you don't have time to recover from this incident. You feel like you're about to have a heart attack.

9. Finally See Sherrie Levine Naked!

You are having an argument with art critic Ben Johnson in the MoMA members' café. He is interviewing you for a cover feature in *Art Vibe!* and begins by suggesting that the 2008 show at Tate Modern *Duchamp, Man Ray, Picabia* must have kick-started your transformation from street artist to gallery star. You respond by explaining that modernist work of this stripe should be handled in exactly the same way that Wittgenstein advocated treating philosophy: as a ladder which is to be thrown away after we've used it to reach a conceptual understanding of the world. Duchamp was right when he said works of art died and ended up in tombs called museums. You add that there is no better illustration of this than Duchamp's own work. You patiently explain that at the age of ten you would have been excited by Dadaist pranks, but by the time you'd reached your late teens you'd moved way beyond them. No mature artist needs to look at Duchamp, they continually reabsorb his influence through his imitators...

Your shaver is your secret vibrator. Discover why men like you are different to all others. Our remedies are proven to be effective and will enable you to add inches to your cock. They will teach you to speak Greek and live in harmony with 2 wives. You will gain an amazing 10–20% in girth after just a few weeks. Challenge your genes! The effect lasts for up to 72 hours after you stop taking the pills. Free trial sample available.

We will send you before and after pictures as proof!!! Get Sarah Lucas naked and wet! Increase your manhood size! Become bigger, longer and harder today! Don't believe those jerks who claim size doesn't matter—to a woman like Sarah Lucas it means EVERYTHING!

Johnson is offended and tells you that you can't criticise Duchamp because all his works are blue-chip classics, and simultaneously function as the foundation stones of artistic modernism. You order another double espresso and tell Johnson to chill out, because if Duchamp were around today he'd agree with you. Then you placate the critic by offering to show him some interesting sex imagery on the web. Johnson hands over his laptop, which is his first mistake, and you go to Flickr. At first Johnson isn't impressed but when you show him Flickr groups like 'Public Nudity', 'Nude Insider' and 'Nude Photographer, Nude Models Contacts' he changes his tune. Of course, you save the best until last, so when you introduce Johnson to the Flickr group 'Sex Contacts UK' he is virtually coming in his pants. This group is dominated by horny transsexuals who just love to suck cock, and is a wet dream to the *Art Vibe!* critic. While you're at it, you click through to a scam site and infect Johnson's computer with viruses that will cause his computer to spew forth penis enlargement spam. Then you make your excuses and leave...

Wondercum! The new medication revolution that will change sex lives worldwide. Volume enhancers used to be dodgy affairs with no real guarantees, but the new miracle-product Wondercum now promises:

1. Longer, harder, more powerful orgasms to drive your lover crazy with desire.

2. Up to 3–4 times more semen per ejaculation.

3. Ejaculations increased 2–3 times in both intensity and length. Sex will never be the same again with the 100% guaranteed effects of Wondercum! Try the revolutionary new Wondercum now—satisfaction assured. Get rock hard for longer!

10. Give Judy Chicago the Best Orgasms Ever!

You receive a message from top critic Ben Johnson telling you he knows a hot little slut who is desperate to make it with knickerless curators from major art institutions, and even better, she doesn't know the difference between the real thing and an assistant curator! Moments later Ben instant messages you to say the minx is actually waiting for you outside the MoMA bookshop, and instructs you to get your knickers off quick and get down there coz she's up for fucking you right now in one of the MoMA toilets! You work in an open plan office, so you sneak into the khazi to whip off your boxer shorts.

Watch Andrea Fraser come again and again. Twins take it up the ass. Andrea Fraser likes to be taken hard and penetrated deeply and fully! Gain an amazing 1 to 3 inches today! High rollers and their prostitutes! Andrea Fraser and top international curator in leaked porn tape. Hit me baby one more time! 'Special' vids of Andrea Fraser! Hello! I am bored this evening. I am a horny art slut who wants to 'chat' with you. Email me at andrea.fraser@g-stringmail.com only! I am using Ralph Rugoff's email to write this. Contact me to see my pics and sizzling hot sex videos! New Swiss Rolex watches at great discounts! Order your luxury timepieces today! Cartier Roadster watches! Andrea Fraser sex tapes available! Your problems solved with our brand new revolutionary product!

You lock yourself in a cubicle and step out of your boxer shorts. You have just pulled your trousers up and your hand is on the flies when your phone rings. You tug hurriedly at the flies so that you can catch the call. As you yank the fly up the skin of your penis gets zippered up with it. You are in agony. From the next cubicle you can hear the Suicide Kid. He is leaving you a message: 'Oh hi Time Server, it's the Sucide Kid, I just called so that we could talk through some more details about my show *Lederhosen Kamikaze Death Squad!*' You start to scream. the Suicide Kid looks up over the divide between the cubicles. He's put the seat down on the toilet in his cubicle and is standing on it.

VPXL is guaranteed to add inches within just a few weeks. Voted the most effective male enlargement supplement by *FHM* readers: As well as permanent, massive gains to length, you can also expect:

1. 20–30% gains in girth.

2. Longer sexual performance with a permanent erection.

3. More spunk when you come. Satisfaction guaranteed. Don't hesitate! Try the only medically endorsed herbal enlargement supplement today! Click here.

The Suicide Kid offers to help you. You hear him emerging from his cubicle. You keep yours locked. You try to pull down your fly. The zip is stuck, it isn't moving and as you pull on it the pain is agonising. You open the cubicle door and ask the Suicide Kid for help. He tells you to lie flat on the floor. As the Suicide Kid adjusts a tripod on which he's mounted a digital video camera, he explains that he'd been in the toilets filming gay men through the glory holes. The camera lens is now behind your head and pointing at your manhood. The Suicide

Kid positions himself between your knees, his camera is behind your head, he wrenches your fly and the zip comes loose. You scream and faint.

11. Lay Mona Hatoum Now With your Brand New Pecker!

You are squatting between the Time Server's legs explaining to the camera on the tripod behind his head how you used Ben Johnson's laptop as a Trojan Horse to trick the Time Server into doing himself an injury. Pretending to be the art critic whose ID you'd hijacked, you sent the assistant curator messages claiming there was an art slut in the building desperate to fuck knickerless cultural bureaucrats. You hid in the glory hole riddled toilets closest to the Time Server's office and belled him on his mobile just as he was about to do his flies up. The skin from his cock caught in the zip as he hurried to catch the phone call...

How much do men really talk about bad experiences in bed? I couldn't believe that in 2 short months, I gained 2+ inches! Be a lethal weapon in the bedroom. Be the MAN you always wanted to be! Stop dreaming about being 9 inches long, and make it a reality! Just take these herbal pills regularly and see results in less than 2 months! Be a member of the Big Boys Club! Give Billie Sellman a mind-blowing orgasm! Want to know how? Want to have the best sex of your life? The power within you is about to be unleashed. Thousands have benefited from this—now it's YOUR turn.

You take your camera from its tripod and get some hand-held close ups of the Time Server's injury. His cock is bruised but nonetheless you consider him something of a pussy to have fainted from what is ultimately a minor injury. You put the camera back on the tripod, then position it a metre from the Timer Server's feet. You're going for the reverse shot with Time Server's head at the back and top of the picture. You turn on a cold tap, cup your hands to catch the water, then throw it over the Time Server's face. He moans as he regains consciousness.

Real penis enlargement! Gain 3.5+ inches in length! 100% safe to take, with NO side effects. Rise from the dead, ye little head...Searching for the lowest priced software? Look no further! With our discounts you can afford the software you've always wanted! Get legal software at the best prices ever! Live the life of a Casanova when you add 3 inches and gain a massive schlong! Thick, long, and rock hard erections, EVERY SINGLE NIGHT—thanks to this miracle solution!

You position yourself behind the camera ready to shift it if the Time Server starts thrashing around. You ask him if he wants you to call an ambulance. He seems to be in shock but says no. You help him up; as he rises his trousers fall down. It's all caught on camera. After pulling his breeks back up, the Time Server carefully positions his dick before doing up the flies. He moves slowly and in exaggerated steps as he retreats to a cubicle. He puts the toilet seat down and lowers himself onto it. He tells you he'll be OK and that you can go; he kicks his cubicle door shut. You noisily slam the main door to the toilet and walk back to the cubicle you'd previously occupied to get more shots of the Time Server through its glory holes.

Do you have your own business and require IMMEDIATE cash? A low interest loan—NO STRINGS ATTACHED! Do not worry about approval! Your credit report will not disqualify you! Extra money to spend however you like!

12. Make Miriam Schapiro Tremble With Pleasure!

The Suicide Kid brought you back to consciousness by throwing water in your face. After this you sit in a toilet cubicle trying to regain your composure. Your injury reminds you of being a child. You must have been seven or eight years old. You were with friends playing on some old garage roofs on the edge of the abandoned Brooklands car racing track near Weybridge. Your feet went through the roof on either side of a beam, smashing your balls against the rusting iron work before you fell down onto the concrete floor. One of the other children present went and fetched your mother. She came with her bicycle and pushed you home sitting side saddle so that you didn't hurt your balls any more. You couldn't walk. Your mother was afraid you'd castrated yourself but she wouldn't take you to the doctor because that would mean explaining how the accident happened, and owning up to the fact that when she'd let you out alone you'd gone trespassing.

Blow Louise Lawler's mind! Your anaconda will finally be deemed Swamp Thing. Exciting nights will be a reality! Andrea Fraser and Rebecca Horn will both come so much faster once you've gained 3 inches! Get a bigger shlong! Get a Captain Fantastic body part! Enlarge, lengthen, and thicken your manhood within a few short weeks. Your instrument works best when it's BIG! A Chris Kraus pleasing immense cock hulky dick growth and girth is GUARANTEED. Robert Mapplethorpe would be proud of your appendage! Amazing growth in just a few short weeks can be yours! Give Vanessa Beecroft a ride on your ROCKET! Boost your confidence with your new-found instrument!

Your mobile phone rings. It's the Suicide Kid. He tells you that you've got five minutes to get yourself together for a meeting with Ian Breakwell. You wonder how on earth the Suicide Kid could possibly know this. Breakwell faked his own death so that he could get on with making art in peace, away from the distractions of the culture industry. You are one of perhaps six people who know this, all of whom are sworn to deep secrecy. You thank the Suicide Kid and tell him that you want to see him later. He agrees to meet you in MoMA's members' café once he's worked his way around the museum's Neoist retrospective.

No more complaints about the pea-sized patheticness of your weenie weener! Solve all your dick-related issues at once! Big dick equals more self-confidence, get it by clicking here. What are you up to? Hello! I'm bored today. I'm a horny art slut who wants to have sex with you. Email me at andrea.fraser@g-stringmail.com only. I am using Hans Ulrich Obrist's email to write this. Would you mind if I sent you some of my nude pictures? Could you send me before and after photos of your soon to be legendary huge schlong? In 2 weeks you can see surprising results. Success is certain. Make the bulge in your pants grow and grow!

Ian Breakwell greets you by saying: 'Hello possum, what are you doing here? Why aren't you dead? I'd heard that MoMA has you chasing your tail the whole time, so you just aren't able to apply for a full blown curator's job elsewhere. Try suicide, you'll last longer!' Then Ian grins, laughs and slaps you on the back! You like Breakwell but his words hurt you, they are too close to the truth.

13. Your New Enlarged Device Will Make Tracey Emin's Jaw Drop!

You have hijacked both the Time Server's desktop at MoMA and the laptop he uses at home. You control the vertical. You control the horizontal. All the Time Server's mail is being routed through a computer you've set up for this purpose. He has his work cut out dealing with the chaos you're generating. And if he doesn't respond positively to the scam emails that are now flooding through his inbox, then you will do so on his behalf.

Your dealer is giving you an earful on your mobile. Martina Mentrup is unhappy. She thinks you have upset the Time Server, and you may spoil the newly forged relationship between 15 Minutes of Fame, her gallery, and MoMA. You tell her not to worry, the only reason she has a relationship with MoMA is because the institution is interested in your work.

Your bazooka will explode her. Tracey Emin just joined YourSpace. We are notifying you of this because our 'People You Ought To Know' tool discovered you and Tracey are both heterosexual, interested in art and live in London. If you do know Tracey, check out the links below. Instead of checking Tracey out, or rather the fake profile for her you recently set up, you take in Margarita Gluzberg's new show at Paradise Row. The transformation of her style is impressive…Her painting is good too, but it's the drawings that really grab your balls and yank them so hard you want to yelp in pain.

Untitled document. Rely on us to make your intimate life happier! You'll get harder erections with Soft Viagra. Life is a pleasure with Soft Cialis. Win Fiona Banner's favour with Soft Viagra. Make your own sex timetable with Super Viagra. Soft Viagra will save you from sexual death. Find out what everyone is taking and talking about. You know you deserve more. No hassle, no exercises needed, just 2 pills a day for an increase in size. Become bigger, longer and harder right away—find out what a girl REALLY wants. Get it right here, right now. Satisfy Francis Upritchard's Blonde Ambition with the best formula EVER!

You gaze around the white cube and find yourself pondering the question: how should we address the architectural dimension of exhibition making? This raises the additional riddle of why curatorship remained so invisible for much of the twentieth century. But this thought is in turn replaced by another: is there anything you want to steal from this exhibition? The answer is clearly affirmative—you'd love to possess all of Gluzberg's drawings—but you're not a kleptomaniac, you're an artist investigating the aesthetics of theft. *Abstract Literature* is a matter of theft and appropriation. You plan to fill MoMA with items stolen from artists, not necessarily art works, and what you really want to steal from Gluzberg is her collection of rare Northern Soul records. Fuck Art, Let's Dance! You haven't told the Time Server about your commitment to larceny yet because you don't want to freak him out while he is still in a position to pull the plug on your show.

Elizabeth Price loves it huge. The secret to a perfect climax. She wants to be penetrated and taken harder, longer, and tighter. Define your masculine identity. Click now for great deals. Land any art chick you ever wanted with your brand new pecker! Today only up to 70% off our product guaranteed to give you better love-making.

Time Slip: Art, Spirituality & Scamming in the Noughties

What follows is an exchange of messages made on the Friendster social networking site between the Suicide Kid and someone using the name Belle de Jour. The Suicide Kid's cybersex partner claims to be an American woman but some of the personal details 'she' provides about 'herself' differ from those of the high-class call girl who subsequently became infamous for the use of this moniker on the internet. In November 2009, it was revealed that Brooke Magnanti was the previously anonymous author of the Belle de Jour blog and book. Nonetheless, the 'false' details given in the following messages may have been adopted as a disguise, since this does look suspiciously like a dry run for the Belle de Jour blog that first appeared in October 2003, several months after Belle's correspondence with the Suicide Kid was concluded.

From: Belle de Jour
Date: 18 April 2003, 5:22 am
Wink

Hi...your name IS Suicide Kid, right? Or should I call you Kid? 'Wink'

I wanted to respond to your message specifically, since you have packed so much into it.

Well, here goes. Thanks for reading my blog…that shows real interest, and not many actually read others' writings… I appreciate your comments…

'Yeah I looked at your blog about your marriage breaking down, and was thinking about it…but didn't want to comment right away…But to me if the marriage wasn't working for you then it wasn't working, so I think you're doing the right thing since it didn't seem like your husband was likely to change… and something obviously had to change…But doing it can be so hard…just keep pushing forward, you'll get there.'

—It IS so hard to do…he doesn't seem to accept the reality of it. Have you been through this? He keeps saying, 'Let's work on it'…but I HAVE been working on it…for almost twenty-three years! I'm tired. Just want to be me…and free. I feel very selfish right now…my parents/sister…they advise against it with religious and MONETARY reasons…but I am dying here. They don't really understand what it's like living with an alcoholic, and they have never really known ME. Thanks for your positive thoughts.

'Yeah I noticed you were a little older than me, I was born in 1979, and your kids are pretty much grown up but quite a bit younger than me…'

—My youngest son is seven. But his older brother is fifteen and older sister nineteen. I just turned forty-six…but I feel younger now than I have in years. I reached a turning point in my life a year ago, realised I was killing myself with food. Hiding under my fat. I had been stifling my real self for years…avoiding confrontation with my husband, neglecting all my interests and passions…trying to fulfill everyone's expectations except my own. It was killing me. So I stopped!

'I'm not so much looking for wholeness in myself alone as in myself and society. We're social beings, as the metaphysical poet John Donne said: 'No man is an island entire by himself…' But the way I see it, our social nature has been distorted by the capitalist society we live in, so we're all alienated…and I go with much of what Marx laid out on that…'

—Deep thoughts…but I think you are allowing these artificial boundaries to make you feel alienated. I have always been a person who judges by demeanor and respect and (I am not perfect…sometimes I get uncomfortable in certain situations… feel threatened or frightened…if people are dressed in a certain way or acting 'ghetto' and I am alone…I don't want to judge on their appearance…but I have been robbed before, and I get nervous…) I have found people from all social strata, economic levels, 'social standings' etc., to be basically similar. Some are wonderful, honest and accepting…others are just plain jerks. I am willing to give all a chance, and I enjoy getting to know everyone. I learn so much from people…my experience is quite narrow…and friendships such as yours helps to broaden my understanding and acceptance of new ideas and backgrounds.

'I should run as I still got a load to do and I need to sleep eventually. I have real problems getting to bed before 3 am or 4 am in the morning, I've always been a night owl.'

—I also have a bit of trouble with sleeping…usually I am afraid I'll miss out on something really wonderful if I fall asleep… while on my trip to Glasgow, I only slept every other night…I figured I'd make it up when I got back to my 'real life'…Ha ha.

You have obviously read a lot and researched so many political views…I am not a student of such things. I prefer to analyse people. I start to get very paranoid regarding any entity with so much power as a government. I deal better with folks 'one on one'…

I hope you don't think I am taking your comments lightly, I seriously don't know that much about the various theories and writings, and I don't want to sound ignorant. I am always willing and open to discuss them…and become more educated.

Take care, my dear! And enjoy the Weegies! Stand at the top of Buchanan Street, on the steps of the Royal Glasgow Concert Hall, and tell them…Belle says HEY Y'ALL! (nice view from there…wish I could be there too) Don't forget to read my new blog, inspired by you…Belle.

From: Suicide Kid
Date: 18 April 2003, 2:51 pm
Extra lessons

Well so far I've stayed dry in Glasgow. It poured today but after I got to the gallery…The teaching I have to do alongside this show is interesting, but I'm stretching the kids, it's this odd thing with how the culture has gone and I'm like challenging them. No detentions, they're supposed to be adults, but bit of extra one to one teaching in my studio I think Belle if you don't make the grades…Ciao, Suicide Kid.

From : Belle de Jour
Date: 19 April 2003, 7:22 pm

Dear curator, I am practically panting in anticipation of the creative assignment you will no doubt give to me. I might suggest that, until you can procure the couch…I'm quite certain that your desk will serve nicely as a firm, spacious work surface. It is usually at a sufficient height to place the work at just the right position to fully appreciate the nuances and thrills of studying a new topic…encouraging openness and sharing…thrusting deeply into the recesses of my limited experience…to bring out dazzling pulses of energy and creativity…which I never imagined could come out of myself.

Your mastery at leading me to these discoveries is amazing. The lengths to which you go to truly reach me…to spur me on to greater passion…simply burns through my inhibitions, allowing me to fly! My breast tingles with the excitement, and swells to bursting at the thought of you taking me under your wing…'pinning me down a bit' as you said, in order to better set me soaring! Please, elaborate on that method… I am unfamiliar with this kind of instruction, and I do so long to please…Belle.

From: Belle de Jour
Date: 20 April 2003, 8:47 pm
Lesson #2: The Desk

Sense perception…is that my topic? Alright.

As I enter your studio, I feel the atmosphere of excitement and enticement. Suddenly I cannot stand the restrictions these artificial bindings called clothes are placing upon us.

To properly delve into our subject, all obstacles need to be removed, to bare our true selves for observation and exploration. The study of each other's anatomies. As you help me to divest myself from my restrictions...I perceive that part of YOUR anatomy begs my immediate attention. In fact...this is a most impressive and upstanding educational tool. All of my senses are required to study this rising development.

First, the sense of sight. I observe a lengthening and gradual filling of your flesh. Before my eyes, it stretches and twitches... its colour deepening and I notice ridges that need to be explored in depth...alluring trails to follow...and its texture has smoothed out to a straining fullness...which compels me to the next step in the process...

Touch. My fingers softly stroke along your extensive length... following along the vein from your base to the tip...aaahh— so smooth, as I expected. But warmer and firmer. My next experiment is to measure your girth. I find that by using my forefinger and thumb, I can form a circle and draw it down over the top. My forefinger is not long enough, I fear...I must add my middle finger to encircle you. This is still not quite sufficient, so I must conclude that your girth exceeds the circumference of my grasp. Therefore, I must use both hands. As I wrap my hands around you...I feel the thickness and hardness beneath my fingers. How is this possible, when the encasing skin is so soft and caressable? I thoroughly enjoy feeling this hard shaft, and the tight furry base...just fitting the opened palm of one hand...rolling it through my fingers, feeling the twin globes shift and roll beneath your skin. Some other stimulus is now reaching my attention...

Hearing. I notice a deepening and quickening of your respiration. It seems to have a correlation in tempo to the tempo of my strokes and squeezes. What was that? A low, rumbling sound...a groan perhaps? And I seem to be making some humming-type moans myself...sort of like, 'mmmmmmmm' and a few shaky expelled breaths.

Smell. Along with the above-mentioned sounds, there seems to be a strangely sweet aroma...spicy and salty as well. I sniff the air...trying to gauge its source...I lean in towards you, it is stronger here. I put my face against your skin...the hair on your stomach tickles my nose...even more of that beguiling scent! I follow the trail of the pheromones to their source...your magnificent erection. Now standing even taller due to the ministrations of my hands. I nuzzle my face closer...to better inhale this rich scent...to mark it in my consciousness...I also now smell my own arousal...the combination rising sweetly between us. My mouth is right here now...I simply must...

Taste. I turn my face into you...allowing my tongue to lightly lick along the side, flicking around, to tease the taste of you into my mouth. Mmmmm. I move my hands to the base...so I can find the bottom of that vein...and my tongue follows it all the way up, in one long stroke. At the tip, I see a bead of fluid... It is too tempting, so I touch the tip of my tongue to taste it as well! Aaahhhh, your essence, distilled and dispensed just for me! I lap it eagerly...allowing its sweet and salty taste to whet my appetite. After cleaning out every bit of that treat from the little opening...I decide to see how the head fits my mouth in a tongue-swirling kiss. Lots of lip action here...moulding and testing the resiliency of your fleshy knob. This is very good now...but the motion of your hips is making it difficult to remain focused on just the tip...you grab my hair now... and fill my mouth with your full length. My tongue cannot move, it is cradling you inside my mouth. My lips are stretched around your width...and you begin moving in and out. As you retreat, I can tongue you some...flicking over your head...then you push back...as I grasp your butt to keep me upright...and hold you tightly. Back and forth...then you withdraw...leaving me panting and confused...

You tell me there is more to the lesson, if I will oblige you by lying upon your desk, you will begin MY study...Your turn, Suicide Kid...I mean, curator! By the way, did I make a good grade on this first assignment?

Thank you, curator! Belle.

From: Suicide Kid
Date: 20 April 2003, 9:51 pm
Extra lessons

Belle, we need to spend some time examining sense perception and what is known in philosophy as 'Bertrand Russell's Table'—although we'll use my desk...Now we think we know what my desk is, but it looks like it is a different colour in different lights, and depending on how hard you press down upon it (or are pressed down upon it) then it feels different too...and if you become aroused (and I intend to arouse you) then your perception of my desk as you're pressed against it changes again too. So to really appreciate this you really need to spend a long time lying naked on the desk. To start with I'll need to touch and caress you, brush my lips against you, just tease a little, and we'll move things very slowly along from there so you can really appreciate how your perception of the desk changes as you become increasingly aroused...

From: Belle de Jour
Date: 21 April 2003, 3:18 pm
No subject.

Good afternoon, curator...

Our lesson ended rather abruptly with your cock being pulled from my mouth...(unwillingly I let it go...I had just begun my exercises...) You instructed me to lie upon your desk...

This wooden surface feels very cool and hard and smooth... my ass got chill bumps when I sat down on the edge, and I shivered all over when the skin of my back contacted the cold surface. You take my hands and place them on the edges of the desk, telling me to hold on and not let go or you will be forced to punish me for disobedience. Yes Sir...

You are now going to instruct me in the art of oral stimulation on a woman's body. This is a totally unfamiliar topic for me, and I am exceedingly curious and a bit nervous.

You look at me with such intensity...I start to quiver.

Part 1: Kissing: You stand at my side...your cock pressing tightly against my side, as you lower your head to me. Your breath flows over my skin...and I run my tongue over my lips...my breathing deepens as you lightly brush your lips across mine. I know I moan...I can feel it inside me...vibrating. Back and forth you rub your mouth over mine...sometimes flicking your tongue inside my mouth...teasing me...I want to grab you and pull you in...but I hold on! You bite my lips... this is wonderful...I suck your lip and bite it softly...tonguing it...I don't want to let it go...but you move your mouth toward my ear...aah. This is decadent...that sucking and breathing and nibbling, I feel the sensations down in my cunt. A pulling and twinges of pleasure…

As you work your way to my neck and throat, your bites are growing a bit harder. I squirm a bit…please. I want…

Part 2: My breasts: For this part of the lesson, you position me with my legs hanging off the side of the desk, with you between my spread thighs…your cock is now so close to my heat and my desire starts to coat both of us. But you are still on the outside…rubbing slowly, pressing me down onto the desk. My legs are supported on your strong shoulders, I am totally exposed to you. You lean down to lick my breasts. All around the outside…around and swirling, your hands cupping and holding them gently. You finally lick my nipple… I lunge up against you…but you hold me down. Then you suck hard, with your tongue working around somehow… and your fingers are tormenting my other nipple…pinching and pulling…Sir, I am coming…I am pushing my clit against your cock… anything I can rub against…I am going crazy! Sir, May I Come To You? 'Yes, Belle, of course you may' aaaaahhh! I am bucking under you and you still suck on me…sending pulses to my cunt so hard I feel like I'm falling apart. My hands start to slip away…to touch you…You have swatted me on my ass with a ruler…just as I am peaking. The sharp sting accompanies my cry of pleasure and the throbs of my cum. My body jerks in surprise…the aftershocks of my cum are still making me buck…I quickly grasp the edges of the desk, I'm sorry Sir. May I touch you? 'Yes, Belle, just for a short while'…so I place my hands along your face…looking into your eyes…thank you for that pleasure…may I kiss you, Sir? You lean down to me, since I am unable to rise up…'Yes, Belle.' I grab your neck, and pour my heart into my kiss…I want to give to you everything…

You gently take my hands…kissing them and you let me feel your cock…so wet from my juices…and so hard and huge from your want…I grasp and stroke it until you remove my hands again…'Not yet, Belle.' My hands are on the edge again… Before you move onto the next part, you place nipple clamps on my still sensitive buds…the sensation is almost unbearable, but I strive to remain calm…the chain is cold against my chest, and I shudder in anticipation of the coming demonstration…

Part 3: Licking my pussy: You are now moving your head down to my pussy…taking my legs into your hands and opening me even wider. Just the feel of your breath and the sight of your head down there…what will you do? I feel your mouth biting softly along my thigh. I jump and you hold me down more firmly. I am stuck to the desk now…I can't move. Then I feel your tongue on the lips right between my legs. The softest part of me…being sucked and licked and kissed by my curator. I start to cry, I think. This is so wonderful, I feel so loved. You run your tongue up along my slit, all the way to my hard clit. The warmth of your mouth there drains all my energy…I think I am passing out! Then all the sensation surges into me, and I am flying! You flick your tongue back and forth, and I feel your fingers push into my cunt. I don't know how many…it just feels very full…in and out you push, all the while circling and rubbing my clit. Sir, may I come…'Not yet'…you back off…kissing the top of my thigh. Settling me down with your familiar voice…but your voice makes me get heated up all by itself…you have a very sexy voice…and I start to get more pulses…I am straining to get you back in me…your tongue laps at me, and you come up to my face to share it with me. Tasting myself on your mouth makes me sob…you gave me this pleasure…this intensity.

My pussy is weeping for you now...and you return to my core, and start slow licks, from the bottom to the top. Over and over until I am begging Sir...then you slip your tongue into my cunt, at the same time you stick your finger in my ass. The fullness and burning and sheer intimacy of this sets me on fire. My hands fly to your head to grab your hair...Oh, Master! As I shudder against your body...reacting to my punishment as I also respond to your love-making...I am starting to cum Sir. May I? 'Hold back now'...

You have pulled your head back, and my hands are gripping the desk harder than before. But your finger in my ass is still moving in and out. I feel another probing my cunt...and another still...until it seems your whole hand is buried in me. Pushing and twisting and driving me wild. Then you put your mouth and tongue back on my clit, suckling. My breasts are heavy and burning...I am dying to come...Sir Please PLEASE May I Come To You? 'Okay Belle...now NOW come to me.' I scream my release as I convulse on your face and hands... Oh!!! You continue the pressure, and I can't handle it as I come...I try to push you away... so hard! as I'm coming to you...and you don't stop sucking me...my clit is so tender...Please... somehow...I feel the sensations start to build again... impossible! I haven't really stopped my spasms from the first come when I start again...Sir, I am coming... May I?...'YES BELLE', you pull the chain between my breasts...tugging on my nipples hard...as I start to climax you remove the clamps...and I simply EXPLODE on you. I don't know what I'm doing now...totally out of control...

I hear something...I don't understand...I feel your cock pushing into me...hard. All the way in...I can't catch my breath...Sir...please...please, give me your cum in my mouth...

You pump so fast I am being pounded into the desk, the sound of your thrusts into my soaking pussy is making me faint with pleasure...I am giving you pleasure too...You pull out of me...and turn me to the side again. Open your mouth for me Belle...and thrust into my waiting mouth.

My hands automatically grab you but you don't punish me... I am beyond thought now...I have no choice but to devour you as you devoured me...I want all of you pulsing in my throat. To feel the cum build up from underneath your cock...on my tongue I sense the ripples of your orgasm start...you groan and then your hard strong hands grip my hair. I am coming Belle...as you shoot into my mouth in waves. I feel the hot liquid in my throat and you pull back a bit so I can catch it on my tongue and lips...licking and sucking all of it...Oh. Your groan has made me clench in new shudders of pleasure... I am undone...You are pressed against me, chest heaving and I pull you down onto me, I need your weight on top of me now... Oh, oh hold me down. I am fading out...Keep me anchored safe with you on me. You lower me to the floor...where we collapse together, our breathing raging. I keep having after-shocks and your hands soothe me...stroke me lazily...then you totally relax on me. This is what I crave...you lying here on me—all of you.

O curator...thank you for this beautiful lesson. Your best student, Belle.

From: Suicide Kid
Date: 2 May 2003, 6:37 am
No subject.

Belle, your assignment was so good that I think I need you to repeat it, because it isn't usual to give one-hundred per cent for this type of work, but I feel like you should be getting one-hundred per cent but you'll need to do the exercise at least one more time so that I can be sure...As for the restraints, well I'm not so big on that but I just think if it brings the other person pleasure then that's cool...The quality of your work means it's never far from my mind...The Kid.

From: Belle de Jour
Date: 2 May 2003, 11:13 pm
No previous experience.

Dear Sir

In answer to your request for a review of my previous work... I am afraid I have not much prior experience from which to pull these scenarios...just my feeble imagination.

For example, when I consider what it would be like to be stretched out on your desk...the cool hardness of the wood sticking to my flesh at my shoulders and ass...with you standing in front of me...so intensely studying me... I get jittery.

Your hands might feel my skin quiver when you lightly touch me...my face, my ears...tracing down my neck to my breasts...lingering there...watching them swell and the nipples strain for your further attention. You take my hard buds between your fingers and thumbs...twisting, rolling and pinching...before you finally cup my whole breast, squeezing and moulding them. You lean down to lick me...and suck hard on one, while pulling the other nipple with your fingers over and over. Your tongue swirls and flicks...causing me to grasp your head even closer...oh, teach me more...this is mind-expanding...I never knew the pulses of pleasure here could reach down all the way to my centre...I'm about to come just from you sucking on my tits! My body is twisting up to embrace all of you...so you turn me to wrap my legs around your waist...and you rub your cock up and down along my slit...spreading the moisture all over...I have recently shaved my pussy...so it is smooth...your dick slides gloriously against my clit...nothing is in the way when the ridge at the head of your cock bumps over it...bringing a moan from my lips. As you rub on me...I am trying to get you inside of me, but you say this is a different lesson...you lean to kiss me...taking my mouth deeply with your tongue, I suck it, growing wilder beneath you. I am whimpering...I need you...Your tongue thrusts into me...like I want your cock...and you start to suck my lips...and lick down to my earlobes and neck...I am about to scream...Please, sir...I want...

You draw back...soothing me with your hands...'Belle, we have studied the effects of the desk on your back...now for a frontal lesson'...You take my legs, and gently lower them to the floor...raising me up to stand with you. Your cock is pressing into my belly...as you hold me so close—just feeling each other and kissing and licking and blowing and biting...mmmmmm.

Then you turn me around and run your hands down my arms, from my shoulders to my fingers. While you are pressing against my behind, you start to bend me over the desk...your mouth is biting and licking my back, and it is so erotic that I am reaching around to grab you and pull you into me...but first you take my wetness on your fingers...plunging them into me and drawing it out all over my ass...you rub your cock in long strokes back and forth along the cleft of my ass...I am really getting crazy now...

The cold desk is tormenting my tender nipples...so sensitive after the roughness of your whiskers and the torture of your teeth and tongue on them earlier...you push down on my back, forcing my body and face down, holding me by my neck against the surface...then I feel you right at the entrance of my cunt. Just there...making me wriggle and squirm to get you in deeper...and suddenly you push all the way in! One long hard stroke...and I start to pant. I swear you are hitting my heart...over and over and I can't breathe! Your hands hold my hips now...to steady me as you pound so hard. My hands grip the front of the desk, as I try to push back, reaching for something...I need something...it's so close...I feel this pressure especially when you start to grind around and around...oh, something is happening now...

You reach under me to find my clit...it is so swollen and pulsing with reaction...you circle it over and over as you drive into me...I squeeze my legs together...tightening up those muscles between my legs, because I feel it building up...and I'm afraid I will fly apart, break into a zillion pieces...come undone! Your finger starts to flick over me quickly...this is too intense curator...I don't think I can...aaaahh...AAAAAH haaaa. I have to breathe now...still panting so hard...I need you... As your body starts to quicken its movements...I squeeze even tighter...trying to hold on now...help...I hear your gasp...and a groan as you bury your cock so deep in me...you are holding my ass as tight against you as possible—your balls hot and pressing on my clit as you grind...every inch in as you pulse and push your cum into me. I feel your shudders and pumps, and I explode around you! My cunt convulsing around your cock as you share your gift with me. You rest upon my back...as we learn to inhale...hold it...exhale...settle...hearts pounding, bodies thrumming and jerking with spasms of pleasure. What a wondrous lesson...Thank you, Sir.

What would you have me do next? Please give me an idea...something that is YOUR specialty...so I can become proficient in that area...in order to please you. Thank you for your tutelage...and for allowing me to so freely express myself. Belle.

From: Suicide Kid
Date: 3 May 2003, 9:51 pm
No subject.

Yes, I really liked your account of the third lesson and to give you a clue about where I want to go I think we need to try sex in public places and after that maybe a threesome. I think with a threesome all three participants should be willing to play with each other, so I don't mind if it's a man or a woman, but there must be gay as well as straight sex involved...And yes, I would like to be right behind you...x

From Belle de Jour
Date: 5 May 2003, 12:35 am
Re: Why not?

My assignment (should I choose to accept it...hee hee), is having sex in a public place.

Considering that:
a) I have not HAD sex in over a year, and b) NEVER in a public place! I'm not quite sure I am up to this task. Especially in regards to your extra-credit add-on of a threesome. WAY out of my realm there!

Perhaps I need some education (hints...suggestions... scenarios...ideas that you find provocative...) to give me the necessary background to do justice to this work.

I really don't know the dynamics of gay sex...you know the limitations of my experience. I need to hear what you find titillating and exciting. The fantasies that get you hard and ready...what is your favourite body part to stimulate and/or HAVE stimulated? Please be specific. Please tell me if you like to be licked...or sucked...or bitten. And WHERE... (I like to really personalise these reports...to YOUR tastes...after all, I want a good grade!)

OK, sex in a public place.

Curator...we have gone to a library in order to study and prepare for this assignment. The huge old tables are laden with our books...and the atmosphere is slightly hazy with the dust motes hanging in the late afternoon sunlight. Our eyes are tired from our research...and I notice your shoulders look tense. So I walk behind you to massage you. I rub deeply and rhythmically up from between your shoulder blades, to the tops of your delts, to the base of your skull...your head leans back against my breasts, and I love the feel of it there. My arms gently squeeze my breasts to enfold you, and I feel your hand reach the back of my knee, rubbing up and down my leg, as my hands begin to rub down to your chest. I circle your nipples through your shirt...making them stand up for me. Your hands have now come up to my neck, and you pull me around for a kiss. We have to be very quiet here in this corner...Occasionally we can hear the footsteps of fellow patrons walking past the end of the aisle. If we attract their attention, they could glance down the aisle and see us.

Your kiss begins with a lick across my lips…I love that. I want to suck your lip into my mouth…tonguing it and nibbling on it. Your tongue dips in…swirls and teases…makes me want it in other places…click, click, click…footsteps approaching… I pull back and you pull me to your side, pushing me down on the other side of your chair, away from the view of the aisle. I see your bulge, and I know what you want. I slowly run my hand over your cock…and release it for my inspection. You grab a book, to hide your erection from the sight of the people passing by. I stroke gently up and down…holding lightly and pumping you with fast light movements. You start to breathe a little jerkily, and someone at the shelves looks over. He cannot see me…but you notice his regard and flash a strained grin at him as I start to lick up the side of your cock. I scoot around in front of your chair now…I need more access to you…so I am under the table now, if anyone cares to notice…

I am now steadily eating you…sucking and really going at it…the book you hold is shielding my head and your dick, but not my body, as I writhe in my efforts to swallow you… oh, you are large…I want all of you in my mouth…tap, tap, tap, tap…quick footsteps…but they pass by…we both have tensed up…the tip of your cock barely in my mouth…so I look up at you while I lick the tip…mmmm…now what do you want?

You push back from the table…and come under it with me…the legs from the other chairs somewhat hide us…you push my skirt up and make me lie face down, my ass held up to you…you slide in…I am already so wet…and you push me all the way down and lie fully on me…grinding up and down…fast and so hard…I manage to get a hand beneath me, and I am fingering my clit desperately! I know we are both grunting, and trying to finish…suddenly I see jeans and boots appear at the side of our table...the guy leans down and sees us! He grins...and starts rubbing his crotch. You don't even hesitate...you keep on pumping as I try to turn over...I don't know what kind of signal passes between you guys...but he reaches out to squeeze my breast, while he keeps rubbing himself. I know I squeak...as you both pull me from under the table...back next to the wall.

He has now replaced you...he has pushed into me, holding hard to my hips. I am so embarrassed...but you tell me it's alright...as you guide your cock into my mouth again. I taste my desire on you...and I am now being fucked by two men... I can't believe it. He starts to finger my clit, and I feel you reaching over to touch him. You are touching his dick as it slides in and out of me. He gets more excited and really pounds into me, forcing my face into you more quickly...I am losing my control...I feel like I'm falling. His fingers are bringing me to climax...and I feel you begin to pulse inside my mouth. He leans over to kiss you passionately. I want that kiss too. As I come I moan...and that sets you both off...I am being squeezed between your bodies. And we all collapse. The kisses continue ...between the three of us...tasting each others' bodies... tongues, and cocks and cunt. You react first...helping to straighten my clothes...the guy is sitting against the wall, his cock still out...panting a bit.

You have already regained your customary nonchalance, when a woman appears at the end of the aisle...she announces the library will be closing in five minutes. She seems to crane her head to see what the man and I are doing, sitting on the floor behind the table...but she just walks on. I help him get settled, and get a final kiss, as I feel you come behind me and you reach between my legs...for one more taste of our encounter on your fingers...we take turns sucking your fingers...and share another embrace. I think you know this man...but I'm not sure. He gets his bag and strolls off. And you and I head back to our car. The questions are burning in my mind. How did that happen?

You help me see the beauty in sharing our bodies...baring our selves...to enlighten our senses. Well, curator, how did I do? Belle.

From: Suicide Kid
Date: 10 May 2003, 3:32 pm
No subject

Next assignment same as the first...Do it again, repetition is the basis of all thought, and all pornography too! x

From Belle de Jour
Date: 10 May 2003, 9:27 pm
Re: Re: Unquestionably...

Oooh...I can TELL you're more than 'able'...wow! I wish we could sit in the back of a cinema...and neck during the sexy parts of a film...which are many...and cuddle during the bloody, violent parts...which are more...but beautifully done...Then just go out to the car...and...well, finish up what we started...have a little 'dessert' after we had 'dined in HELL'...

My appetiser would be your cock...licking around to taste every inch. The glaze on the tip being the special sauce! I would have to suck every drop and squeeze and stroke you...but perhaps there is somewhere else your cock should spray its glaze upon...I stand outside behind the open door of the car…with you behind me. You lift my skirt just enough…then shove your way into my soaking pussy…fast…faster! We are parked at the back of the lot…but there are other cars around…

I am practically lying across the seat, pressed down by your arm on my neck and shoulders…your other hand busily fingering my clit…making me squirm and push back hard against your slick cock. You are pounding into me…but I can't scream…my mouth is muffled by the seat…I buck against you…and you feel me build up and spasm on your hardness as you shove as deep as you can…aaaaaahhh…that's so good… I am now about to pass out, I came so hard…blackness swirls at the edges of my vision, and I go limp. You hold me firmly as you now thrust a finger into my ass…you can feel your cock inside my cunt and you finger yourself through my ass. You start to really push hard and faster…groaning as your juice explodes into me so deep. I feel the pulsing and your grinding against my bottom…starting my after-shocks anew. Oh Suicide Kid…it feels so good.

People are walking towards us now…you hastily close your pants…and pull my skirt down, urging me to my feet. I almost crumple, but you hold me up with your hands on my ass, I grab your neck. Our combined juices are running down my legs, and a couple glances over to see our embrace. The man notices the wetness glistening on my skin…the woman pulls him toward their car as he hesitates. You are biting my neck…making a mark of your possession, your conquest…your victory. I know I am whimpering…and suddenly you howl out…making the woman grab her escort and demand his attention…I think we may have started something there…

Well, it's probably time to drive back home…looks like time for a bath, hmmmmm? Belle.

From: Suicide Kid
Date: 4 June 2003, 2:17 pm
No subject

You got me hummin' (misprint)...

From: Belle de Jour
Date: 4 June 2003, 2:37 p.m
No subject

Hum against me...give me those groovy vibrations...

Mmmmmmmmmmmmmmmmmmmmmmmmmmm, Belle.

From: Belle de Jour
Date: 7 June 2003, 5:18 pm
No subject

I am mmmmmisssing the mmmmmmmmmotion of your mmmmmmmmmmouth hummmmmmmmmmming against mmmmmmmmmy mmmmmmmmmmmalleable mmmmmmmmammmmmmmay and mmmmmmmmmmy tummmmmmmmmmy and mmmmmmmmeet mmmmmmmme in Mmmmmmmmmmemmmmmphis, baby!

'I couldn't think up an 'm' word for pussy...but THAT would be rather mmmmmmmmemmmmorable too! He he.' Love, Belle.

From: Suicide Kid
Date: 8 June 2003, 9:53 pm
No subject

Mmmmmmmmmmmmmmmmmmmmmmmmmmmmmmm
mmmmmmmmmmmmmmmmmmmmmmmmmmmmm.

Mmmmmmmmmmmmmmmmmmmmmmmmmmmmmmm
mmmmmmmmmmmmmmmmmmmmmmmmmmmmm.

Mmmmmmmmmmmmmmmmmmmmmmmmmmmmmmm
mmmmmmmmmmmmmmmmmmmmmmmmmmmmm.

Mmmmmmmmmmmmmmmmmmmmmmmmmmmmmmm
mmmmmmmmmmmmmmmmmmmmmmmmmmmmm.

Mmmmmmmmmmmmmmm. x

Before Birth: The Curator

14. Find Out How John Lennon Got Yoko Ono Pregnant!

You are not impressed by MoMA's Neoist show. There is too much work by Stiletto and Vittore Baroni, and hardly anything by equally central figures such as Pete Horobin and Blaster Al Ackerman. The curators have obviously gone for what they feel looks slick rather than presenting a representative selection of eighties underground art. Likewise too much of the show is made up of post-Neoist material of the 1990s created by groups such as the London Psychogeographical Association, Association of Autonomous Astronauts and Decadent Action. Indeed, the later material is treated as if it is Neoist, and this really angers you!

Wonderful cut price software for Windows and Macs. Get great discounts on popular software today! All software is instantly available thru our download system. No need to wait! OUR SOFTWARE COMES IN ALL EUROPEAN LANGUAGES—American-English (USA, Canada, Russia, China, Tibet, Borneo, Korea, Iceland, Greenland etc.), British-English (England, Wales, Kernow, Mannin, Scotland, Greater Scandinavian Isles of Orkney and Shetland, Channel Islands, Norway, Sweden, Denmark, Australia, South Africa, India etc.), French, Italian, Spanish, German, Polish, Finnish, Estonian and more!!! Windows Vista Pro With SP7—$59.95. Adobe Acrobat Pro 19—$69.95. Office 2010 Pro—$59.95. Adobe Photoshop

CS12—$79.95. AutoCAD 2010—$149.95. And we have wonderful software for MACINTOSH too!!! Microsoft Office 2012 for MAC—$79.95. Adobe Acrobat 11 Professional for MAC—$59.95. Adobe Creative Suite 14 Premium for MAC—$229.95. Macromedia Dreamweaver 15 for MAC—$69.95. To review full list of offers, visit—CHEAP SOFTWARE HERE!

You meet the Time Server in the MoMA members' café. He demands to know how you caught wind of his meeting with Ian Breakwell. You tell him you are psychic. The Time Server is silent for the best part of a minute, then he informs you that this is an amazing coincidence because his grandmother was psychic too. You want to laugh but somehow you manage to maintain your composure.

Next Time Server pulls a very old issue of *Frieze* magazine from the bundle of papers on the table before him. He tells you that Nicolas Bourriaud can't possibly be right-wing because he put together a great book list when he did the *Frieze*, *Ideal Syllabus* feature in May 2008. You look at the piece and laugh. Two of the three 'theoretical' books are by John Zerzan and Louis Althusser; respectively an anarcho-numbskull who wants to 'smash' civilisation and a tankie—so these hardly provide Boring Ass with left-wing revolutionary credentials. The rest of the list is equally pathetic, either middle-brow literature or stuff that's popular with juveniles—among the authors Boring Ass rates, that you read way back when as a teenager, are Vladimir Nabokov, Richard Brautigan, Fyodor Dostoevsky, J. K. Huysmans and Raymond Roussel. Once you've stopped laughing, the Time Server insists that the footage you took of him in the toilet be destroyed. You've already transferred it to your laptop, so you let him wipe it from your camera.

Boner™ is the only supplement proven to add 4 inches to your manhood. Nineteen separate scientific studies have concluded that Boner™ is the only medical answer to male size issues. I was unable to make Rut Blees Luxemburg come, but since I've gotten thicker and longer with Boner™, she has multiple orgasms every single night.

15. Take our Herbal Remedies and Surprise Faith Ringgold With your New Length!

You try to explain to MoMA's CEO Gail Litvinov, that you are not responsible for the emails spewing from your computer, messages that are bringing the museum into disrepute. You have been targeted by computer hackers and the information technology department are so busy that they aren't able to come and clean up your hard drive for three months. Litvinov doesn't seem to be listening to you, as far as she's concerned the buck has to stop somewhere, and she's decided it is to be with you. Gail orders you to fess up to being under stress, admit you deliberately sent the offending emails and to draft an apology to all your contacts, which she's to approve before it is sent.

Give your lady total satisfaction! Extra length is easy, it's just like ABC http://www.tonyduffer.com. 3% discount. Coupon #7859. Dear Time Server, be wise, purchase your pharmaceuticals from the best shop since 2000. Give her more of your rod! It is basic psychology that a girl loves a guy with a mightier weapon of desire: http://www.tonyduffer.com. Ask us to award you one of our PhDs. Enjoy a prosperous future, increase your money earning power, and earn the respect of everyone around you. Bachelors, Masters and PhDs available in all fields. Professional and affordable!! Call us on 1-010-101-

0101. It has never been so easy to radically change your life. Good times await you when you buy our herbal growth pills. Get yourself an art school girl. Get your giant pilot into Clunie Reid's cockpit.

You sit at your desk and try to compose a letter of apology. The words just don't seem to come into your head or flow from your fingers. You ask those around you for help. They think the idea of taking personal responsibility for the spam email is stupid. One of the interns says she'll write the email for you. She can touch type and within ten minutes she's bounced the missive across to your terminal. In it you apologise for the spam spewing from your computer and castigate the hacker who is responsible for their sexism. You talk about the glass ceiling in the art world, about how the majority of gallery goers are women, and how male artists and curators still dominate the top of the profession. The hacker who has infected your computer is clearly intent on the continuation of this inequitable situation, which feminist artists have laboured long and hard to redress.

Carry yourself with confidence when you gain a new huge schlong. Never hear another complaint about your small weener. Buy Cialis online. THE LOWEST Cialis PRICE GUARANTEED. Other, less serious side effects may occur. Continue to take tadalafil and talk to your doctor if you experience CHEAP CIALIS ONLINE. Autumn Discounts, BUY IT HERE! Want it cheap? Get it cheap from India! Regain TOTAL confidence in yourself with our herbal remedies! As soon as you get this, you will forget all your worries. Make every night a memorable night! Freak Vicky Gold out with your gigantic SCHLONG! Great experiences start here!

Gail Litvinov replies to you almost immediately. She's happy with your apology despite the content being at variance with what she told you to write. That said, Gail figures you don't have the intelligence to have composed the text you sent her, so she assumes one of the female interns helped you with it. Litvinov concludes her missive with praise, saying effective delegation is the key to good management.

16. Fiona Rae is Lovin' It! Lots of Action Awaits you in her Barbican Bedroom!

You have been stitched up like a kipper. You turn up for the unveiling of a commissioned work you produced to be temporarily sited in Limehouse Town Hall, only to find that overnight a group of illustration students from a local college have erected substandard pieces of their own around your installation. Visitors assume that the student work is a part of your commission and some of them are sniggering at works that have nothing to do with you.

Due to an enormous increase in the volume of our business we are moving to larger premises. Our other exciting news is that we are having a MOVING SALE, from today until July 15th. To take advantage of the AMAZING discounts on all the pharmaceuticals we stock, order today! If you order by July 15th you will receive a 37% discount—AND you will also get 10 FREE bonus pills with each order. This is a HUGE DEAL! You won't find bargains like this anywhere else, so don't delay ORDER TODAY! HURRY to our site and stock up for a whole year. We are here to serve your pharmaceutical needs. You too can add 3 inches to your manhood in just a few weeks! http://www.jacksonpollock.com.

You demand that the student work be removed but are told that the owners of the building can put whatever they like in it. The students responsible for this slop have also been invited to attend your opening to swell the ranks, since one of the Commission Commision's major patrons, Lady Michelle de Grimston, is giving a speech. Your anger subsides a little when you're told you'll be financially compensated as long as you hang around for the speeches and the dinner afterwards. You agree after noticing that one of the students is a cute redhead, and she's invited to the meal as your companion.

Chris Kraus can't wait for night to fall once you have this. Never hear any more complaints about your small weener. Let Ceal Floyer feel more of you. Get your new huge dick here. Leave Louise Wilson speechless with your legendary new cock. Change your garden tool into a POWER DRILL. Solve all your dick-related issues at once by clicking here. Big thick dick equals more self-confidence. Get Rut Blees Luxemburg into the sack by clicking here. Realise all Marine Hugonnier's sexual dreams by clicking here.

Lady Michelle de Grimston turns out to be the daughter of a long distance lorry driver, and was born and grew up in Grimsby. Back in the nineteen eighties she was working as a hostess in a gentlemen's club when an aging member of the aristocracy proposed marriage. She accepted and less than five years later inherited the old lecher's fortune. Michelle places her hand on your knee under the dinner table. You'd hoped to cop off with the cute redheaded student, but you know what's good for your career and resign yourself to going home with Lady de Grimston.

Non-stop action every night—do you have what it takes? Tired of losing your erection in 15 minutes, or of having a small schlong? Here is the solution. There will be no stopping you after this! Your powers are soon to be unleashed! Give Diane Arbus what she wants with your long hard instrument!

17. Carolee Schneemann Kisses and Tells! You Can Achieve Natural, Maximum Gains!

You are working on a follow-up to MoMA's highly successful Neoist retrospective. The institution's ongoing interest in Neoism is something you wish to keep quiet until you have secured the loan and purchase of further work. Unfortunately a virus on your computer is decrypting and then mailing out secret draft documents from what is supposed to be the secure section of your hard drive. Not just your computer but your entire life is being overrun by spam.

Hello dear, I guess you won't be surprised to receive my mail? I saw your profile and it is great to know you are doing well. Do you remember when I put you in the same correspondence novel as Rod Summers VEC/RAF back in 1984? I'd like to resume our previous fun relationship. I am no longer Oz by name, and online I call myself Rebecca. No kids and still single according to this profile, despite having fathered a dozen kids in my other gender. I would like to know what you think about my death? You can contact me at this email address rebeccaneo666@yahoo.com. Reply and I will send you some of my fake pictures (hey these are worth seeing since I got a cute 19 year old to pose for them). Remember old Neoists never die, they just delete themselves from history. Reply soon, Rebecca.

Time Server at MoMA London is proud to present innumerable works by David 'Oz' Zack, the man who founded the International Neoist Network in 1978. There are many rumours concerning the fate of Zack, a man who devoted himself to the art of story telling. From 1992 onwards various versions of Zack's death have circulated in Neoist circles. At the core of all the stories is the contention that Zack fell ill after being imprisoned in Mexico, but details vary. One story has it that Zack failed to report the deaths of his parents to the authorities; that he kept their mummified bodies in his basement, and continued to collect their pensions.

Other tales suggest other forms of welfare fraud, including claims for non-existent dependent children. A further variant on these stories is the suggestion that Zack was jailed for debt, and failing to meet court ordered maintenance payments for dependent children. Some tales relating to Zack's imprisonment include the claim that due to harsh conditions and lack of insulin to keep his diabetes in check, he lost a leg. Upon release Zack is supposed to have travelled to Texas where he was nursed by Blaster Al Ackerman's wife Patsy, leading to the break-up of his best friend's marriage. Shortly after Ackerman departed for a new life in Baltimore, Zack is alleged to have died.

Never make another credit card payment. Join the thousands of art world insiders getting out of debt. Be debt free in as little as 12 months. Visit the link below and get a free debt consultation today. NO OBLIGATION! http://davidozzack.com.

Zack is known to have obsessed over the disappearance of noted Dadaist and amateur boxer Arthur Cravan off the coast of Mexico, as well as the fate of writer Ambrose Bierce who disappeared during Mexican Revolution. Both Cravan and Bierce have been put forward as the actual author of the mysterious B. Traven novels, and these works also fascinated Zack. Given such interests, and the discrepancies in the various accounts of Zack's mysterious demise, a number of commentators have suggested that he faked his own death and is, in fact, very much alive.

18. Find Out Why Rebecca Horn Can't Get Enough! Effective Results Immediately!

You are attempting to explain to the critic Kevin Callan the purpose of your computer art. Among the many works you've created are thousands of appropriated penis enlargement spam emails in which you've replaced generic references to girls, women and ladies, with the names of famous female artists. Thus 'She'll scream in pain once you have a huge cock!' becomes 'Lee Miller will scream in pain once you have a huge cock!' Of course, much of the spam was originally composed by hacks who speak English as a second language; you had to rewrite it to make it harder hitting and more effective. That said, by replacing generic terms with the names of real women—and occasionally gay men—you're making explicit the envy and unrealisable desires that consumer society stimulates in all of us.

Sarah Lucas will scream in pain once you have a huge cock! Lovin' her and giving her pleasure will never be the same again, once you have a titanic extension! Don't let your love life suffer because your weener is tiny—you can put on inches with this quick and simple solution! Porkin' Sarah Lucas and making her come will be a piece of piss once you have a GIGANTIC schlong! Special prices, 2012 winter offer! Regain TOTAL confidence in yourself with THIS! Next big market winner. We told you to add Nigerian Art Insurers to your watch list. Up 4 straight days with record volume. The underlying prices are constantly increasing and policy issues have hit an all time high. Load up on Nigerian Art Insurers shares!

Callan complains that your work is demeaning to the women featured in it. You counter that it draws attention to the way in which their work is devalued by a patriarchal capitalist society that views art activities and more specifically the role of the artist, as one of the few legitimate areas of male emotionality. You understand that everyone reproduces their own alienation within consumer societies and that to participate in the art world is to become implicated in every aspect of it, including massive amounts of discrimination against all those who are unable to construct themselves as centred white male bourgeois subjects. Callan accuses you of sounding as if you'd like to abolish art, and you agree with him. In a sane world, art as we currently know it would not exist!

Superstar art report. Neoist art prices are at an all time high. We have THE undiscovered gems of the Neoist underground art movement of the nineteen-eighties. We have works by David Zack, Blaster Al Ackerman, John Berndt, Michael Tolson, Pete Horobin, Vittore Baroni, Kiki Bonbon, R. U. Sevol, Graf Haufen, Arthur Berkoff and many many more!

The Neoist movement recently received an OFFICIAL exhibition at the Museum of Modern Art London and prices have been rising steeply ever since. Combine that with a PR campaign and flood of positive news and Neoism is almost guaranteed to hit the price levels already paid for Dadaist and Surrealist productions of the 1920s and 1930s by artists such as Marcel Duchamp and René Magritte. That could mean a spectacular profit of 2,000% if you buy Neoist art works from us now! Neoism is not a fly-by-night art movement, there is real talent and very real opportunity. Even with selling pressure on the art market the prices paid for Neoist works is up 40% this week. Which goes to show, you cannot keep a good underground art movement down. Get in on NEOISM NOW! CLICK HERE!

19. Your Fantastic Device Will Make Andy Warhol Shake! 70% Off Penis Growth Pills!

You are re-reading the notes the Suicide Kid is preparing to accompany his exhibition and you're not happy with them. One thing you most definitely object to is the suggestion that Andrea Fraser's *Untitled* (2003) is an art prank. Fraser, who is well-known for practising institutional critique, asked the Friedrich Petzel Gallery to find a private collector who'd pay around $20,000 to have sex with her as a work of art. The encounter which took place in a hotel room was filmed by a stationary camera without sound and with the male participant's face remaining obscured throughout. You appreciate that the resulting unedited sixty-minute document is a classic of relational aesthetics, whereas the Suicide Kid has the temerity to suggest that the reason the male participant remains anonymous is because he isn't a private collector at all, but one of Fraser's boyfriends. You don't understand how anybody could suggest such an important work of art is fraudulent.

See what's new with Andrea Fraser at artworlddateline.com. Andrea has added new friends—http://artworlddateline.com/friends.php?uid. Andrea has received new comments—http://artworlddateline.com/phpaf. Want Andrea to know what you've been up to? Join Andrea's network—http://artworlddateline.com/user.php.911. Joining Andrea Fraser's network instantly added 1 inch in length to your penis!

Participating in Andrea Fraser's Art World Dateline network will turn your maggot into a monster! Don't you think it's degrading when they call your dick a 'baby carrot'? Don't let them make fun of you anymore! Use Andrea Fraser's network to permanently increase your penis size! Give it a try and make those who mock you kneel in worship before your huge new male meat!

You feel anger boiling up from the pit of your stomach as you read through what the Suicide Kid has sent you. He has the nerve to berate Andrea Fraser for reviving what he insultingly describes as 'long ago discredited idealist bunk about the critical autonomy of art'. When you studied Adorno and the Frankfurt School at university, you couldn't understand what they meant by the critical autonomy of art, so it is clearly ridiculous for a young whippersnapper like the Suicide Kid to claim the notion is discredited. Besides, if you allow this nonsense to accompany a show you curate, it will undoubtedly damage your chances of assisting Andrea Fraser in the creation of a future work of art grounded in institutional critique.

Hello dear! I don't imagine this email will come as much of a surprise to you. I found your profile here on Art World Dateline and you sound like my kind of guy. I propose a mutual exchange of pleasure in the pursuit of art. My name is Andrea True. No kids and still single. I would like you to meet me in a hotel room, where you will fuck me senseless with the entire encounter being filmed. You will pay me $20,000 for the privilege and I will sell the resultant work in an edition of 10 for the sum of $100,000 each. I will give you one free copy and keep all money from sales. This is a once in a lifetime opportunity for you. You can contact me here on Art World Dateline and if you are interested, I can send you my pictures and more information on the post-Frankfurt School approach to institutional critique. Have a great day but please rush your reply to me because I am sitting at home feeling bored and lonely. I'm dripping wet just thinking about fucking you. Give me more, more, more! Andrea True.

20. Georgina Starr Will Never Laugh At You Again! Add More Inches To Your Male Shaft!

You have spent three days working flat out on a proposal for an exhibition at The Mile High Studios in Hammersmith, west London. *The Realisation and Suppression of 100 Years of Feminist Art* will fox your critics by providing you with a route through which you can return to painting. You've already made a few of the works. Most notable among these is a painted realisation of the *Venus de Rokeby* by Velázquez after its feminist modification and improvement by Mary 'The Slasher' Richardson in 1914. That this was the direct inspiration for much of the work of Lucio Fontana is rarely acknowledged by art critics. However, rather than slashing the canvas, you have painted the slashes onto it to replicate Mary Richardson's improvements.

If you have undergraduates who find it difficult to write a decent term paper, or postgraduates who are having problems with their theses or publications, we may be able to help you. We offer a personalised, online, tutoring service, designed to help students and academics produce solid well-argued texts that are fit for their intended purpose and appropriate for their intellectual discourse community, whether it be feminist art history or underground cultural movements of the 1980s such as Neoism and The Church of the SubGenius. So, contact us with a troublesome text and we'll return it to you with a free preliminary analysis in 24–48 hours. Best regards, David Zack: http://www.davidozzack.com.

With regard to the attack on the *Venus de Rokeby*, Mary Richardson made the following statement: 'I have tried to destroy the picture of the most beautiful woman in mythological history as a protest against the Government for destroying Mrs Pankhurst, who is the most beautiful character in modern history. Justice is an element of beauty as much as colour and outline on canvas. Mrs Pankhurst seeks to procure justice for womanhood, and for this she is being slowly murdered by a Government of Iscariot politicians. If there is an outcry against my deed, let every one remember that such an outcry is an hypocrisy so long as they allow the destruction of Mrs Pankhurst and other beautiful living women, and that until the public cease to countenance human destruction the stones cast against me for the destruction of this picture are each an evidence against them of artistic as well as moral and political humbug and hypocrisy.'

Superstar art report. Art is worth far more than its weight in gold! The contemporary art market is on fire! If you want old masters we also offer a cut price faking service which for a small surcharge includes certificates of authentification! It is also a proven fact that the value of paintings rises dramatically if they are attacked. The resultant publicity ensures vandalised works rocket in price. We offer an all-in-one vandalism and restoration service. Smarties really are loading up on underground art of the nineteen eighties, and in particular all things Neoist. If you missed out on Fluxus and Conceptual Art when that could still be bought for a song, or the post-modern blue-chip names of the nineteen eighties like Cindy Sherman, don't miss out on Neoism!!! Despite fear of recession in other world economic markets there is no need to despair when you can safely invest your wealth in Neoism, and pile up massive immediate gains! Get into Neoism and reap the profits! Don't delay, contact us today! Best Regards David Zack. http://www.davidozzack.com.

21. Sue Webster Will Love It When You Enter Her With Your New Found Size!

Amidst all the junk messages that are pouring through your inbox, you missed an email that appears to be from David Zack. He is willing to assist you in your plans for a major retrospective of his work, and also wonders if you could put him up (and cover the air fare) if he flew to London to help you. He also tells you about a forthcoming retrospective show devoted to his work in Canada, but begs you not to let the organisers know that he is alive and well and in direct contact with you.

Authentic David 'Oz' Zack style paintings with appropriate markings in the correct place on the canvas. The subliminal seductions worked into the painting are guaranteed to make women jump into your bed; these include hidden words amongst the abstract swirls such as 'sex', 'fuck' and 'orgasm'. Paintings made with the same automatic hand movements employed by Zack. Includes genuine reproduction David 'Oz' Zack signature, produced by transfer from facsimile of an original, this signature is a feature of all genuine David 'Oz' Zack paintings. All appropriate David 'Oz' Zack style markings in the correct places. Made using genuine jazz drummer's hand movements to drip the paint, just like the original David 'Oz' Zack paintings. http://davidozzack.com.

One message David Zack forwards to you reads as follows: 'Greetings groovy people! It fills me with joy to announce that a new David Zack show will open at The Neo Gallery (TNG) in Calgary, 26 November 2012. It will be an installation focusing on Zack's work from the 1970s and 1980s. The show is based on Pete Horobin's archival collection with the addition of holdings from many other sources. Right now I'm editing a documentary film about Zack based on Super 8 and video footage taken of him in Dundee (Scotland) in 1986, A catalogue will be published to accompany the show. There will be room in the exhibition for additional contributions sent by those who wish to add something. Yours for the Neoist Revolution, Monty Cantsin. P.S. Never Make A Credit Card Payment Again—visit http://www.davidozzack.com.

With a bigger penis you'll get to lay as many art sluts as David 'Oz' Zack! It is derogatory when Gillian Wearing calls your package a 'baby carrot'? Don't let Sophie Calle mock you anymore! Use VPXL to increase the length and girth of your trouser mouse! Order it today and get ready to hear more complimentary descriptions of your new huge male meat! All The Pills You Need! You may not believe that within one short month, you can add an inch in length to your small penis! Seeing is believing! Rush your credit card details to: http://www.davidozzack.com.

You can't believe your luck. The real David Zack is going to help you with your retrospective show of his work, thereby ensuring that it is the best exhibition of his paintings ever! You exchange a few emails and before the day is through you're buying Zack a train ticket from Baltimore to New York, and from there a flight to London. You do this using his alias of John Berndt. You now know that Zack had to fake his own death due to various difficulties he'd experienced with the US authorities and afterwards he took on the identity of a fellow Neoist called Pego Berndt. He has however sent you an affidavit from Blaster Al Ackerman confirming he is indeed David Zack.

22. Show Rachel Whiteread an Amazing Time in Bed With our Special Pills!

The Book of European and American Neo-Neoism! Due to the spectacular demand for Volumes 1–6 of *The Book of European and American Neo-Neoism* (each with its own bonus CD) all of which were presented sequentially starting with Volume 1 at the 30th, 31st, 32nd, 33rd and 34th International Book Art Fair in Buenos Aires (Argentina), *The End of the World*, 1st Biennial, Ushuaia (Argentina), *Arte Clásico*, Lawyers School, Buenos Aires (Argentina), International Cuenca Biennial (Ecuador), and many other major international art world events, we are continuing to spread the names and the work of the artists included in these tomes on a world-historical scale.

Thanks to our attention to detail and the wide diffusion of our publications around the globe, the featured artists have been invited to diverse cultural events of major significance and all have verified the presence of all volumes of *The Book of European and American Neo-Neoism* in all museum, gallery and private collections of any significance whatsoever around the world.

We are renewing our call for the *The Book of European and American Neo-Neoism*, Volume 7 (for which we have secured the participation of visual artists from Spain, Portugal, France, Costa Rica, Peru, Turkey, United States, Chile, Uruguay, Brazil, Mexico and Argentina among others). We have selected your work on the basis of what's displayed on your internet website.

If you wish to participate, just ask for more information: http://www.davidozzack.com/bookofneoism.

Remember that this is a non-commercial educational project. In order to include you in *The Book of European and American Neo-Neoism,* Volume 7, we need you to sign a contract agreeing to the costs of publication being split between you and all the other selected artists. We can, however, guarantee that you will be able to secure inclusion in *The Book of European and American Neo-Neoism* for not more than $500, and possibly far less if you can persuade all your artist friends to participate as well.

The concept of the book: Pages of text taking the form of short biographies or curricula vitae or comments (no more than thirty lines in English and thirty lines in Spanish). This entices curators and researchers to look at your work. You can include a web link so that people can immediately find pictures of your work online. Unfortunately prohibitive costs prevent us from including illustrations in these books, which are given away free.

Format: 200 x 290 mm. Full colour, laminated cover. Each artist will receive five copies of the book for free and need only cover postage costs to receive them! We will also mail books to cultural and educational institutions including museums, libraries and art colleges in both Argentina and around the world!

BOOKS SHELTER OUR DREAMS & ENSURE THAT THEY DON'T DIE OF COLD!

For more information and a further breakdown of costs check http://www.davidozzack.com/bookofneoism.

23. Nan Goldin Will Give you Head Every Single Night When you're A Large Nine Inches!

Good day Sir/Madam. On 21 June 2012 at about 9.00 am, the world witnessed a natural disaster. A quake measuring 9.0 on the Richter Scale occurred in the Nevada Desert close to The David Zack Depository of twentieth and twenty-first century art.

The quake destroyed The David Zack Depository buildings and ruined thousands of examples of blue-chip art. This is a disaster unprecedented in scale in the whole of human history, and leaves the destruction of the Library of Alexandria (once the largest library in the world) looking like no more than a mild case of foxing on an otherwise tasty first edition of *Das Kapital* by Karl Marx. Reports say this was the strongest quake in the area for 4,000 years; its energy output was equal to 9,500 Hiroshima atomic bombs.

So far 155,000 works on paper have been officially recorded as missing, and of this figure, 277 are by Pete Horobin, 79,900 by David Zack himself, and 27,268 by Blaster Al Ackerman. Fluxus works recorded as missing number 6,000 and there are over 10,000 missing mail art artefacts from the former Eastern bloc. The Swedish Prime Minister says about 1,000 works by Swedish artists are unaccounted for, and if pieces by Danish artists who lived in southern Sweden for at least part of their career are added in, then this figure must be revised dramatically upwards!

The art world has so far donated twenty-one million pounds towards rescue and restoration of these works, with ten million raised overnight. Various City of London hedge funds specialising in art have also pledged fifteen million pounds;

the EU has pledged four million US dollars and other international organisations are pledging sums of money to save what can be rescued of this invaluable collection of art.

Your financial contribution towards getting art restorers and a building team (which are the most important needs) are vital to our success in preserving what we can of David Zack's cultural treasures. Please send your contributions/donations no matter how small, via WESTERN UNION MONEY TRANSFER to me, David Zack at: zack@davidozzack.com.

Please endeavour to let me have full information about the payment of your donation. By this means I will be able to send you a tax-deductible receipt redeemable in most developed countries (excluding Iceland and Moldovia). I therefore need the following from you when you send your donation: amount paid, your name, your bank account number and sort code, your address, secret question with answer for verification purposes only.

For sums exceeding four thousand euros, please mail me immediately for my private bank account information: zack@davidozzack.com. Please note that no sum is too small or too large to donate towards this worthy cause. Please consider this humanitarian plea as urgent and give as generously as you can. Thank you in advance for donating money to help save cultural artefacts that are utterly priceless including many major and important works from the mail art and Neoist networks. May God bless you as you donate. Yours faithfully, David 'Oz' Zack.

24. Blow Faith Wilding Away With Your Enlarged Prick!

You arrive for a meeting at the MoMA project space expecting to talk to the Time Server but are instead confronted by representatives from the Health and Safety Departments of both the museum and the local council. They want to know exactly what you will be doing during your show, and when you suggest you may want to black out the gallery for short intervals, they completely freak out. You are told you can't black out the gallery and if you want to darken it you must have MoMA staff members in attendance with powerful torches and backlighting.

Never be flaccid! Have mind-blowing sex at last with the extra inch of manhood we will help you attain: http://www.akademgorod.com. Beautiful naked art sluts are lusting for your company! Christine Borland won't be able to get enough of the action you'll give her every night: http://www.blasteralackerman.com. Discover the best-kept secret online! Louise Lawler will give physical shape to your fantasies in a way you can never forget http://www.davidozzack.com. Martha Rosler's dreams will come true! Guaranteed increase in penis size experienced by 90% of our test subjects http://www.montycantsin.com.

Then Health and Safety pop the all-important question. Will there be any nudity? You reply that there may be nude pictures and that you might want to take your clothes off during performances inside your installation. Health and Safety say you must have signs warning people that the exhibition contains material of an adult nature, to prevent families with children wandering in. They ask if the audience will be seated during your performances and insist that if they are, then any chairs used must be fixed together and placed in rows of five.

The latest breakthrough in enhancement science is finally here: PollockGain+. Proven conclusively in multiple studies conducted around the world to increase male length by at least 2 inches in just weeks. Average gain exceeded 3 inches. Increase width, musculature and thickness by at least 15%. Amazing increase in volume of spunk produced when you ejaculate. Intense, wave-like multiple orgasms achieved. Top art sluts including Tracey Emin and Karen Finley have expressed immense satisfaction with the results. The increase in size gained by male partner from PollockGain+ helped them achieve climax almost three times more often. Never Mind The Jacksons, Don't Blame It On The Boogie, Here's The PollockGain+! Now available online for a limited period—get yours while stocks last! Visit http://www.jacksonpillock.com.

The discussion with Health and Safety moves on to the question of fire. You explain that you won't be using fire in the gallery but that as part of the performances on the opening night you will be having a barbecue on the stone patio immediately outside the gallery. Health and Safety tell you the fire must be professionally supervised at all times and properly damped down at the end to avoid it flaring up after everyone has gone home, which might result in the stone work becoming cracked and thus lead to someone injuring themselves upon it. When you volunteer the information you were planning to burn some books by the likes of Nicolas Bourriaud, Health and Safety freak out. They nix the idea saying that controlling the temperature of burning books is virtually impossible, and you will generate too much heat.

25. Even Katarzyna Józefowicz Will Give Out Once you Enlarge Your Manhood!

Our safe, secure games will get you smiling. Download our casino in 20 seconds to get $999 richer when you join. Relax and have fun with poker, blackjack, roulette and progressive video slots! 'I Won't Raise Taxes', says Schwarzenegger, 'Except For The Indians!' How To Break Up With Your Girl, Then Get Some Bootie Time! http://davidozzack.com/sex. Three sexy teens fuck one lucky guy hardcore foursome! Two extremely hot lesbians making out and getting ready to screw!! Arnold Schwarzenegger to make movie! Viagra is the answer to women on antidepressants and helps them regain their active sexual lifestyle http://www.davidozzack.com/topnews.html. Britney pays $20,000 for custody! London air pollution index rises, Olympics cancelled.

You arrive at the London MoMA project space to begin installing the Abstract Literature exhibition and are greeted with sullen looks and much silence. You've been trying to get on with your work for about thirty minutes when the police arrive. You are arrested for computer hacking and fraudulently awarding yourself a prestigious art exhibition by pretending that you were two different people. You protest that this is ridiculous and waste your one phone call attempting to contact the Suicide Kid. He isn't picking up the phone.

This is an email enquiry. I wonder if you are interested in selling text link ad space on your page here: http://www.stewarthomesociety.org/libri.htm. Feel free to email me back at neoistdatingsites@gmail.com. Thanks. Dear Customer, for your security, the portfolio that you are using to access Zack Internet Banking has been locked because of too many failed log on attempts. We urgently request you to follow the link below to unlock your Internet Banking: http://www.davidzackonlinebanking.com. We guarantee to refund your money in the unlikely event you experience a fraud with your internet banking. Regards, David Zack Online Security Department. Young London! A nice girl wants to get acquainted with you: http://neoistbrides.com.

The cops call in a doctor and he performs various psychiatric tests. You see the results were pre-written; his notes existed prior to the start of the session. You're a paranoid schizophrenic with delusions of grandeur. The claim isn't based on tests, it is a fit up. How could you possibly be both the Suicide Kid and the Time Server? They're like chalk and cheese, opposites that simultaneously attract and repel each other! It's like travelling from Ism to Jism and back again...If you read this as the Time Server, then you were being taught to speed-read, now go back and read the whole book again.

89% OFF Pfizer! About this mailing: you are receiving this email because you subscribed to David Zack Featured Offers. David Zack respects your privacy. If you do not wish to receive David Zack Featured Offers email, please click the 'unsubscribe' link below. This will not unsubscribe you from email communications from third-party advertisers that may appear in David Zack Featured Offers. This shall not constitute an offer by David Zack. David Zack shall not be responsible or liable for the advertisers' content nor any of the goods or service advertised. Prices and item availability subject to change without notice. © 2012 David Zack.

26. Karen Finley's Used G-Strings and Yams For Sale!

Fine Arts Insurance for Collectors & Dealers. If you are having trouble viewing this message, please go to http://nigerianartinsurance.org, for special deals brought to you by Nigerian Insurance Services, Idi Amin & Sons, 69 John Coltrane Square, Abuja 10009-2112, Federal Republic of Nigeria—http://www.idiamin.com.

Good news! After 29 years in the insurance business we have partnered up with Nigerian Art Insurance Company and Nigerian Insurance Company. We can now negotiate favourable terms and conditions with very competitive pricing. We have the facility to insure all collection types and sizes, dealers, museums and non-profit galleries.

If you are involved in the art world, I can insure your exposure: commercial art; art and antique dealers; restorers and conservators; museums; private collectors; large or small inventories; domestic or international; art fair transportation, while at fair, shipped to collectors; art loaned to museums or non-profit organisations; art being shipped or carried on board; coverage for special events, parties, galas, dinners; charities and more!

There are special policies so broad that besides the standard theft or breakage coverage it actually includes mould and devaluation of the art pieces due to turbulent trading conditions! The premiums begin around $2,500 for about $250,000 worth of protection. Recent successes: an art dealer who brings works to various fairs and sells from her private gallery just purchased this policy: $300,000 premises limit, $300,000 unnamed location, $300,000 while in transit! We set the unnamed location limit and transit limit as matching limits to avoid any gaps in coverage. Premium is $3,100 with $1,000 deductible.

The genuine article! Total flexibility with market-leading security; the ultimate high-net worth cover for art and antiques, collectables, buildings and contents. Call me with your questions. Idi Amin, CIC 212 404-7878 ext 69—idi@idiamin.com.

Dealer Insurance: http://idiamin.com/dealer.pdf
Museum Insurance: http://idiamin.com/museum.pdf
Corporate/Private Fine Art and Collectibles Insurance: http://idiamin.com/fineart.pdf

We also offer top quality Wyndham Lewis drawings! Get top quality Vorticist drawings, reproductions and copies: http://idiamin.com/forge. Authorised dealer of prestigious luxury & fine Wyndham Lewis art works with 70% off! Other artists available include Pablo Picasso, Marcel Duchamp, Joseph Beuys, Andy Warhol, Asger Jorn, and Charles Thomson. If you don't see the artists you're looking for in our lists just ask! Famous name artists at discount prices! Email us with your requirements.

And while you're on our site why not try our no hassle business loans? If you have your own business and want immediate money to spend any which way you want then our no strings attached low interest loans will astound you! Don't worry about approval, your credit history won't disqualify you! http://idiamin.com/$$$.

Appendix: Stewart Home Replies to an Enquiry from Guardian Newspaper Blogger Jane Perrone Concerning the Claim that he is the Real Author of the Belle de Jour Blog and Book

Hi Jane

Given that I'm quite used to people making bizarre allegations about me and that in any case I advocate radical ambiguity, I don't really see that there is any point to denying or confirming that I'm Belle de Jour. Since I'm supposed to be 'a liar' it is pointless for me to deny that I'm Belle, as this will only serve to confirm it for those who want to believe that I am. Likewise, if I claim to be Belle this will be accepted as proof by those who want to believe it's me, and taken as a denial by those who favour rival theories. Remaining silent serves me no better either since some of those who want to believe I'm Belle will insist that I'd never admit authorship, but my refusal to deny it will be taken proof that I am responsible. I can't win, or rather, I can't loose. My advice to anyone at all interested in the identity of Belle is that they buy all my books and pour over them looking for clues as to whether or not the blog and book might be my work. Personally I attribute Belle to the current anti-social state of social relations.

I'm no more interested in who Belle 'really is' than I am interested in who Jack the Ripper 'really' was. The endless speculation about the identity of such figures serves only to obscure any understanding of them. That said, for purely personal reasons I would be interested to know the identity of Jack the Stripper, who murdered six west London prostitutes in 1963—64 (or at least eight over a longer period depending on which position you take on who the victims were). The nude murders are covered in depth in *Found Naked And Dead* by Brian McConnell (New English Library, London 1974). I understand that next year Granta are publishing a book by David Seabrook that will take a fresh look at Jack the Stripper and west London prostitution in the sixties.

The controversy about Belle reminds me of the scandal surrounding the publication of *The Story of O* in France in the fifties and sixties. In fact, no one correctly identified the author at the time of that controversy. That said, other books about London prostitutes are perhaps more instructive in this instance. *Streetwalker* by Anonymous (Gramercy Publishing, New York 1962, there was an earlier British edition) strikes me as just as likely to have been written by a man as the female prostitute narrator. There is something very fake about the book and I view it as a work of fiction. The same might be said of *Jungle West 11* by Majbritt Morrison (Tandem Books, London 1964). While Morrison appears to have existed she was probably unable to produce a convincing account of her personal experiences because she received too much useful advice about content from an editor who was keen to help her write a best-seller. So while there is a grain of truth to

Jungle West 11, it remains a Notting Hill classic of fiction much more than of fact, taking us primly through various forms of prostitution from streetwalker to call girl to club hostess. Similarly, there are at least three ghost written 'autobiographies' by Christine Keeler: *Nothing But Christine Keeler* ghosted by Sandy Fawkes (New English Library, Sevenoaks 1983); *Scandal!* (Xanadu, London 1989); and *The Truth At Last* ghosted by Douglas Thompson (Pan Books, London 2002).

Instead of worrying about who Belle might or might not be, it is considerably more interesting to look at why the chattering classes prefer fixating on the identity of a latter day 'happy hooker' to examining the economic realities that force many women into this 'profession' (and here it would be useful to return to Marx and his use of prostitution as a metaphor for capitalist exploitation, as I did in my novel *Down & Out in Shoreditch & Hoxton*). I should also add that prostitution is just a job, a way of earning money for those women (and men) engaged in it—an economic and not a moral choice. Most prostitutes are single mothers or have a drug habit to support. Naturally, I view being a prostitute as infinitely more honourable than being a cop, a politician, a soldier or indeed a butcher.

Moving on, I've no idea who produced the document you emailed which identifies me as Belle, but I assume it was done as a hoax since it mixes genuine information about me with utterly spurious assertions. Of the anonymous documents mentioned as being produced by me, some were and some were not my work. Since I circulate such tracts to disrupt the activities of reactionaries, I prefer not to identify what I've done since to do so reduces its effectiveness.

Likewise, my mother Julia Callan-Thompson did in fact work at Murray's in the early sixties, then at Churchill's (a similar establishment) through the mid-sixties. This is not a hoax as is asserted in the document. Such disinformation is hardly going to help me with the ongoing research I'm doing into my mother's death, although I'm sure whoever concocted it doesn't really care about the fact that I would like to know how my mother died. What they've done only serves to cloud matters about my mother and while Paul Knapman (the coroner who dealt with her death) has responded politely to my letters about it, I do not feel he has been particularly helpful. I view this document as adding grist to his mill and not mine.

I also found it strange that the document listed *Suspect Device* (an anthology of short stories authored by diverse hands, that I edited), as one of my novels but omitted another of my books *Whips & Furs: My Life as a Bon Vivant, Gambler & Love Rat* (Attack Books, London 2000) which for the purposes of public circulation was attributed to Jesus H. Christ. It would seem that whoever put this document together was either careless or else they know less about me than they'd like others to believe.

I hope this clarifies matters for you. I can elaborate on some of this if you'd like me to. It is too long since someone last took me to lunch at St John Restaurant or even the Quality Chop House...and so if you haven't used up your expenses by the end of the month, it would be one way of doing so.

Ciao, Stewart.[1]

1. This email was first published in full on the *Guardian* website on 11 April 2005. The week before the *Evening Standard* newspaper ran the claim that Stewart Home was the 'real' author of the Belle de Jour book and blog in its print edition.

Selected Comments from a Stewart Home 'Mister Trippy' Blog, Entitled *King Mob's Chris Gray RIP*, Posted on 19 May 2009

b says: 25 May 2009, 11:32 pm

As you well know, Stewart, it's all about money... That's why Debord made *Society of the Spectacle* into a film (an absolutely classic cash-in), and that's why you wrote the Belle de Jour books. And yes, some of us are NOT so stupid as not to have realised a very long time ago...

Maybe if you keep trying you'll make as much money as the *Q* crap-arses did—what a bunch of fucking-wanker self-publicists. Yeah, that's just what the proletariat needs. Now they're selling pseudo-ironic pro-Americanism (Cary Grant), and get the trendy intelligentsia to copy their pseudo-ironic style. They don't mean it, you know, they didn't get into publishing on Umberto Eco's coat-tails. God, what a case of 'the emperor has no clothes'. The middlings all follow suit and look down their noses at people who say 'what a load of shit' as being terribly common and unsophisticated. Pretty much the same tool being used as the one you yourself have wielded so deftly really...

...You are one of the top recuperators of previous-generations' radical stuff in the land. Which is why you especially singled out the Wise brothers to slag off in your intro. The Wise brothers are honest and decent; you aren't.

So Gray wrote a book about acid. Who's the old fool again?

mistertrippy says: 26 May 2009, 12:08 am

The (Not So) Wise brothers may or may not aim to be decent and honest, but the reality is they are well-meaning but nonetheless self-righteous and deluded. Personally I've never aspired to being decent, but it is almost too decent of you to pay me the backhanded compliment of saying I am 'one of the top recuperators'. Which has about as much 'truth' as saying I wrote the Belle de Jour books. The (Not So) Wise circle is so easy to wind up it is boring.

b says: 26 May 2009, 12:49 am

Oh Christ, the guy's putting 'truth' in inverted commas...What hope for someone like me who puts some value in the concept, against an opponent like that? But then for you I suppose everything's literature. I called you 'one of the top recuperators of previous-generations' radical stuff in the land'. You are. But it's a very niche role. (As with most of what else I've said here, this won't be news to you in the slightest). Capitalism doesn't have much call for recuperating such stuff at the moment, and probably never will do. You're no Felix Dennis when it comes to business sense, not even a Naomi Klein (maybe if you had the same religion you'd have climbed further?), but what with the Belle effort you must be worth high six figures I'd say.[2] And whilst those books are not notable at all (anyone sensible ignores them just as they ignore 99.999% of the rest of the here-today gone-tomorrow chewing-gum water-cooler bestseller-list shit), the skills you used were honed in recuperation...What I said...

2. Although I dislike the circulation of racists slurs. I'm leaving one here, as it was posted on the blog, because it reveals how bigotry and conspiracy theories twist minds.

As for your joking about the Wise brothers' surname. Sophisticated. Maybe it'll catch on? Nothing like a little bit of sugar to help the poison go down.

Personally I think it's good to be decent, and haven't got much problem with self-righteousness either. You know you're twisting.

But enough. You're a fucking liar...

b says: 26 May 2009, 12:50 am

What goodness is there in calling someone an entrepreneur, to your idiot market who take you seriously, when you are someone who's not an entrepreneur and never has been? I'd call that more the action of a cunt.

mistertrippy says: 26 May 2009, 9:13 am

Better to be a cunt like me than a anti-semitic fool like you. You keep claiming I wrote the Belle de Jour books, but you've yet to provide any evidence for this. You just keep repeating the claim and seem to think this will prevent people from noticing you haven't substantiated it...I appear to have wound you up.

Selected Comments from a Stewart Home 'Mister Trippy' Blog, Entitled *More on the Death of Chris Gray*, Posted on 25 May 2009

b says: 26 May 2009, 12:29 am

...I won't tell you how many people know about the Belle de Jour thing...(more than you think, I suspect), but there you go.

mistertrippy says: 26 May 2009 at 12.46 am

So what makes this true other than the fact you keep repeating it? Read it in the *Evening Standard* did you? I did too but that doesn't mean I believe it. You remind me of the Devon and Cornwall cops who read in the *Big Issue* that Jimmy Cauty had a stash of weapons, so they went and raided him, only to find there was nothing there.

b says: 26 May 2009, 12:56 am

You left huge tracks both before and afterwards—advice to asiring writers, loads and loads of stuff—and actually it was me who clued in the guy who gave the story to the *Evening Standard*. You think you know it all but you'd be surprised how many people can see right through you on this one.

b says: 26 May 2009, 1:21 am

The guy who gave the story to the *Evening Standard* (if he got paid, it wasn't much) and his fellow early-times litto-blogger originally thought it was Lisa Hilton—you know, that posh totty who you put out disinformation about (ha ha!), before the *Evening Standard* had the story and without your even thinking ANYONE would be clever enough to suss you were 'Belle'...So no, to answer your question, I didn't get it from the *Standard*.

mistertrippy says: 26 May 2009, 11:56 am

None of which provides any evidence for the unsubstantiated claim you've repeated on this thread that I am the author of the Belle de Jour book and blogs. I suggested on the other thread about Chris that it would be useful if you attempted to substantiate your claims on this score.

All you've said so far is: 'You left huge tracks both before and afterwards—advice to asiring (sic) writers, loads and loads of stuff'. What advice? Where is it? How does it prove I wrote the Belle de Jour book and blogs? The idea I've given 'advice to asiring (sic) writers' is in itself ridiculous. My advice to anyone wishing to be a professional writer would be not to have children, rather than to sire them.

Ricardo Terrori says: 26 May 2009, 1:05 pm

I read about the Belle de Jour 'mystery' like four years ago in *BuzzWords*, I think, definitely not at the *Evening Standard*. I don't remember if I have read some of it, but I still don't see what the point is if Stewart writes it or not, even if he says he doesn't.

Did the collective name thingy and stuff amount to nothing?

Are we returning to the disgusting Respect For Identity times? C'mon!

Muammar Al-Gaddafi 'wrote' it, boys! (In fact, him, chief recuperator on his land, plagiarised it from Fanny Hill… on acid).

mistertrippy says: 26 May 2009, 2:38 pm

Rick, I've got no interest at all in who wrote the Belle de Jour texts, but if people are going to make claims about this and wish to be taken seriously then they should provide some evidence. I don't care if people do or don't think I wrote the Belle de Jour book and blog, what I'm pointing out are epistemological issues. The old fool posting this rot no doubt believes what they are saying is true, but I am less interested in the truth or falsity of the claim than I am in their inability to back up their arguments. As a consequence I would treat everything they say as unreliable, not because I think they are lying, but because they lack the necessary critical skills to make informed judgements.

Maybe you know anyway, but the Mama Soul fan that posted the comment above/beneath you was making a pun. For those that don't, Wikipedia puts it this way:

Joseph Kessel (10 February 1898 – 23 July 1979) was a French journalist and novelist. He was born in Clara, Entre Ríos, Argentina, because of the constant journeys of his father, a Lithuanian doctor of Jewish origin. Joseph Kessel lived the first years of his childhood in Orenburg, Russia, before the family moved to France. He studied in Nice and Paris, and took part in the First World War as an aviator. Kessel wrote several novels and books that were later represented in the cinema, such as *Belle de jour* (by Luis Buñuel in 1967). He was also a member of the Académie française from 1962 to 1979. In 1943 he and his nephew Maurice Druon translated Anna Marly's song *Chant des partisans* into French from its original Russian. The song became one of the anthems of the Free French Forces. Joseph Kessel died in Avernes, Val-d'Oise. He is buried in the Cimetière de Montparnasse in Paris.

Ricardo Terrori says: 26 May 2009, 4:03 pm

Got the evidence argument, Stewart. As you said, people can draw conclusions about quality of the argument. I remember when I wrote an email to you about polemics, what were your methods, etc., and I know you have one of the more impeccable logical skills sets I have ever seen.

Never knew about Kessel. As I stated before, I lost a lot of puns and subtleties, but doing my best while trying to divert attention to my rants about the 'Third World', which 'authenticity' is, at least, unreliable also.

Didn't know of the Buñuel movie either and that's just plain ignorance on my sorry part!

You rock even more when some old fool stirs you up!

P.S. I've got you mentioned on my humble blog, just a little update of what is going on here for a few readers in Spanish language.

b says: 26 May 2009, 5:57 pm

Oh well, I'm back…

You tripped up by publishing advice to aspiring writers under your own name around the same time as doing exactly the same thing under the Belle name, and what parallels there were in the content! I'll leave aside your awfully killing reference to the fact that I made a typo and missed the 'p' out of 'aspiring', and focus on your mealy-mouthed denial of ever having given advice to aspiring writers. In reality you've TAUGHT COURSES TO ASPIRING WRITERS, in which you've encouraged them to, er, set up blogs under false personas. I'll leave it to others to Google this stuff. Made my points. I'm not in court…

As you know (I think you may have been the one who revealed it?) Trocchi did pretty much the same thing with the fake author crap, which job maybe never even got exposed in his lifetime? As Belle you suck up to chosen hacks and cultural figures like no-one's business. You whirl the idiots around your little finger… Of course, what else does one expect? The literature world is a suck-up world—and all your fucking opus is literature, literature, literature. Nothing to get really angry about, this Belle biz. Just thought I'd mention it, is all… Many who read this blog are naive and might as well not waste their time…

b says: 26 May 2009, 6:11 pm

Just for those who were wondering whether they should give any credence to Home's suggestion that I was making stuff up, here's a link to some info on how Home has not only given advice to aspiring writers, but actually held a post where it was his job to do so.

http://melbourne.indymedia.org/news/2007/02/138501.php

He says the idea he advises aspiring writers is ridiculous. Doesn't stop it from being the truth. The rest I'll leave to others to find. He's trying to waste my time by coming over all 'epistemological'. He underestimated the world when he thought no-one would realise he was the author of the Belle stuff. One day he's going to come a cropper…

mistertrippy says: 26 May 2009, 9:00 pm

Looks like I was wrong, you do know you're lying. It stretches credulity too far to credit you with honest intentions when you turn a pun on the word 'siring' (playing off your typo, since you missed the 'p' in 'aspiring' and turned it into 'asiring') into me denying I've ever held a creative writing job. So you've proved that you're a dirty rotten liar. I'm not impressed.

b says: 26 May 2009, 11:46 pm

Trippy—yeah, as always—dish up the shit for the punters to drink up, and then when time gets called, it was a joke all along and only fools would think it was genuine. I mean punning on a typo. Fucking sophisticated, that. Right up your epistemological street.

You know the advice you gave to writers, not to think about success but just to enjoy their work and then success might drop out of the tree as an added bonus? Do you know where I heard that first? From Tony Wilson of Factory Records—the millionaire businessman who bought up some of Debord's art work and then funded a conference discussion to increase the value of his assets. Eat your heart out, Charles Saatchi. As for Dick Pountain, whose name was mentioned here...maybe ask Charlie for his number and see if you can sell an obituary (sorry, aren't I using the publishing-queen lingo? I mean 'obit') of Gray to one of Dennis's publications. That's if Pountain doesn't want to do it himself. Not that any title in Dennis's empire comes to mind as suitable, but you've never been short of business chutzpah.

Some advice you gave in the Belle persona:

http://belledejour-uk.blogspot.com/2007_01_01_belledejour-uk_archive.html

mistertrippy says: 26 May 2009, 11:51 pm

Have you always been this boring or is it just something you've got into lately?

b says: 26 May 2009, 11:56 pm

You ask THAT, after penning the verbiage of the preceding post?! 'Anything less would be a failure to break with bourgeois modes of thought and shallow rationalism.' 'Break with', indeed. Ping! Switch on the enlightenment! But I'll leave you to your 'interesting' colleagues in literary London and bullshit bloggery...

Ricardo Terrori says: 27 May 2009, 1:38 am

The fake author is not crap. It is not even an author, but that story is as old as literature. Think of 'The Bible', written by ghost writers of 'GOD'.

I'm not an aspiring writer, thanks Horus, but I have awful headaches and take a lot of aspirin, which has my poor stomach quite damaged.

In an experimental spirit, although, I have Googled the folllowing tags:

Stewart Home courses aspiring writers blogs false personas

...and got an astonishingly limited number of answers; amongst them, the most interesting turned out to be my own blog, CRAFT, then and a page of an ex MI6 agent claiming to be an aspiring writer, and six collages by Out To Lunch.

Didn't get anything about situationism or Bhagwan.

I'm naive and want to stay this way.

Who says we all must to be revolutionaries, or even writers?

...DOWN WITH AUTHENTICITY!

LONG LIVE BULLSHIT BLOGGERY!

resentful ideological knickers says: 27 May 2009, 5:13 am

b, Mr Home has really got to you hasn't he? His success writing about Situationist works clearly really pisses you off...

But you really are getting your resentful ideological knickers and union jack pants in a twist about nothing—who cares if S. Home did, or didn't write such and such a book, did or didn't do what he said he did?

Who cares if he is toying with, subverting, using the system or playing along with its contradictions?

Who the f*** cares? Haven't you got better things to do with your time? Lots of good books to read, friends to make, whatever.

Good luck! There is a whole world out there to explore...

Michael Roth says: 27 May 2009, 4:01 pm

...I still have a few questions—

Why is it so important for Stewart Home to have written the Belle de Jour blog? Is there some significance that I'm missing if he did write it? Is there some sort of reward or prize if we can prove who in fact is the Belle? Does anyone actually care about this anymore?

...Why does b have a crush on Stewart Home? (and I mean that creepy, stalker-type crush.)

Why does b sound suspiciously like my girlfriend? (and if b is my girlfriend, I will take out the garbage LATER, OK.)

Well, I think that's it for now...

Yes, The Bozos who Claimed I Was Belle de Jour Were Completely Deluded! Stewart Home 'Mister Trippy' Blog. Posted on 17 November 2009

A thirty-four year old Bristol based research scientist called Dr Brooke Magnanti has outed herself as the 'real' author of the Belle de Jour blog and books. These texts 'documented' the life of a high-class London call girl. Dr Magnanti claims her writing is an authentic record of the time she spent working as a prostitute to fund the final phase of her PhD research. I haven't looked deeply into the various proofs that Dr Magnanti is Belle, but plenty of news journalists have and they seem convinced by them. So while I can't say with absolutely certainty that Dr Magnanti is Belle, it seems to me to be rather unlikely that she isn't.

One thing I am absolutely certain of is that I didn't write the Belle de Jour blog and books despite the claims to the contrary made by various conspiracy nuts. Although the media (most notably the *Evening Standard* and the *Guardian*) ran with this story, it didn't originate with them and I was never under the impression they believed it to be true; they covered the claim without taking any very strong line on it because it made a good story. I benefited from the publicity and sold books as a result, while the journalists in question were paid and generated profits for their bosses.

Curiously, it appears that the majority of those who made and repeated the claim that I was Belle de Jour as if they personally believed it, did so out of spite and malice. It is therefore ironic that their activities helped rather than harmed me. The endless conspiracy theories propagated by these bozos were so ludicrous—involving as they did interminable and utterly fantastic international 'criminal' and 'political' outrages—that no-one took them seriously. It was even claimed that when I temporarily took the position of writer-in-residence at Strathclyde University, I'd 'fled' to Scotland in a vain attempt to avoid arrest by the cops. Despite the linked assertion that my incarceration for endless heinous sex crimes was imminent, I remain at liberty...

In fact, beyond a handful of nutters, no-one who'd looked into the matter ever believed I was Belle de Jour. You only had to compare my prose to Belle's to see that I couldn't possibly have written the tedious shit 'she' spews out. My view of Belle's work is that it is mindless bollocks aimed at middle-class airheads. Had I not been publicly accused of having composed this garbage, I wouldn't have bothered looking at it, and so it shouldn't be necessary to add I would never have bothered writing it. That said, if Dr Magnanti is indeed (as I think likely) Belle, then hats-off to her for evading detection for so long and doing something useful in the area of cancer research. Since her prose is so unappealing, she should quit writing and stick to medical matters instead.

And while you're at it don't forget to check—www.stewarthomesociety.org—you know it makes (no) sense!

110 Responses to 'Yes, The Bozos Who Claimed I Was Belle de Jour Were Completely Deluded!'

Mobile Raver says: 17 November 2009, 1:59 am

At least we know that it was you that wrote the Gnostic Gospels!

Zen Master K says: 17 November 2009, 2:01 am

And *The Complete Works of Shakespeare*...

msmarmitelover says: 17 November 2009, 2:19 am

Belle de Jour wrote *Amputee Sex* didn't she?

Michael Roth says: 17 November 2009, 6:13 am

Stewart (if that is your name??), I never knew that you were a fit bird, and a doctor to boot!

Michael Roth says: 17 November 2009, 6:14 am

I first heard accusations that you were the 'Belle' a few years ago. At the time, of what I knew of your writing/schedule/etc., the claim seemed quite ludicrous. Jump forward a few years and I was again dumbstruck to see the accusations pop up on this blog several months ago or so. If I remember correctly, these accusers really became enraged whenever you denied you were 'Belle', insisting otherwise. I must admit as a spectator, it was very entertaining. I would imagine their red-faced, foaming at the mouth, twisted expressions as they hammered on their keyboards, and laugh to myself. It's these simple pleasures...

arse says: 17 November 2009, 11:07 am

You'd never have done it because of the aesthetics? Because it was bad prose? What, even if it made lots of money? Yeah right. Look at all the shit you spew out. Look at your unscrupulous readiness to play up to the respect your mug readers have for 'news journalists' and 'medical' researchers, which you know as well as any real radical does, are a bunch of pea-brained crawlers working for big business. Cancer research, my arse—generally funded by big tobacco and the food industry and government funding-distributors working for 'em. Magnanti is a shill. What were the international criminal and political allegations, by the way? Never heard of them. Wanted for sex crimes, fled to Scotland? No-one can say you don't keep your image under attentive management. Magnanti is a shill...The prose has your fingerprints all over it...

Joseph Kessel says: 17 November 2009, 11:22 am

I already cured cancer!

mistertrippy says: 17 November 2009, 12:01 pm

Look Michael, here's 'Arse' to entertain you, so you don't need to go looking back at the Chris Gray blogs for a chuckle...And it seems 'Arse' hasn't done his or her research properly because they don't know about the idiots making those allegations in comments all over the web, all linking me to Belle. But perhaps 'Arse' is just pretending, perhaps it's all 'a joke', although if I had his or her mentality (fortunately I don't), then I'd accuse them of being much worse than somebody's useful idiot… Anyway, here's fun for those that in the eighteenth and nineteenth centuries would have paid for admission to a lunatic asylum to be entertained by the crazies…Sings sweetly: 'Conspiracy theory it's such a delusion, conspiracy theory there's too much confusion…'

Mark Nugent says: 17 November 2009, 12:27 pm

The amount of charlatans in society always makes me suspicious of people who claim 'authorship' dubious. Good skewer Stewart.

arse says: 17 November 2009, 12:36 pm

Just the claimers Mark, or the deniers too? God you must be sharp-minded and a man of the world, seeing through charlatans and stuff!

As for those claims, Stewart, so you didn't have a hand in any of them then? Or in producing anything related to Sarah Hilton that even the foolish Andrew Orlowski managed to suss? You take your punters for mugs—and you're right.

fi says: 17 November 2009, 12:48 pm

I dyed my hair raspberry pink today, it looks quite nice actually.

Cassandra Thomas says: 17 November 2009, 1:03 pm

Obviously you weren't Belle. The money didn't show ;-)

Anne Pigalle Bis says: 17 November 2009, 1:13 pm

No, no…I am Belle de Jour (Buñuel style)—I used to hang out in these gardens featured in the intro scene of the film—for real…x

David Flint says: 17 November 2009, 2:18 pm

I'm Belle de Jour and so's my wife!

Tania Glyde says: 17 November 2009, 3:07 pm

I'm actually Belle de Jour and I claim five pounds off myself.

Sean Diamond says: 17 November 2009, 4:29 pm

Funny how all the haters who pop up on here from time to time never seem to have the guts to post their real names. Could the likes of 'b' and 'arse' be Will Self in disguise?

Kate Muir says: 17 November 2009, 7:17 pm

Damn, I wish I was Belle de Jour!

Russell Brand says: 17 November 2009, 7:19 pm

Oh I shagged Belle a few times, even though she's a bit older than the chicks I usually go for.

Christopher Nosnibor says: 17 November 2009, 7:22 pm

What? You'll be telling us you didn't write *Stone Circle* or any of the Harry Potter books next!

The ghost on the coast says: 17 November 2009, 10:10 pm

'Ask not for whom the Belle tolls; ask what you can do for your country.'—J.F. Hemmingway, Secretary of the Inferior, 1939–85.

Paul 'Poland' Rogers says: 17 November 2009, 10:38 pm

I wasn't feeling myself when I left the comments above as arse, who is one of my 666 multiple personalities. I meant to write Lisa Hilton not Sarah Hilton…but then all posh totty looks the same to me, I mean him, my other personality arse. Also I'd like to point out that I, I mean arse or should that be Richard Hunt, made a mistake when they suggested Mobile-Home might have left the comments about having fled to Scotland himself… people might jump from that to the conclusion that perhaps Mobile-Home left the comments from arse and b too, except I know he didn't coz I did in one of my many split-personalities, or I think I did anyway, and if I didn't it must have been Mobile-Home what done it! Oh and I hate Ford Prefect too! And look, I've used my real name, except I'm not really Paul Rogers, I'm, I'm, I'm, well I'm not sure who I am but I know I hate all you mugs who ain't nearly so clever as a conspiracy theorist like me who has seen through all the lies. It's all lies, lies, the media, it's all lies!

The ghost on the coast says: 17 November 2009, 11:03 pm

I thought the law. Can't say it did me any favours.

Half-Baked Moron's b-hind (AKA arse) says: 17 November 2009, 11:39 pm

And Mobile-Home wrote the Old Testament and the Koran, so we should impeach him now. And also he doesn't eat regular meals, or go to church! He has also engaged in fornication out of wedlock. What's more he smells. And he's a nerd. He's a loser. And a wanker! I HATE him, but most of all I HATE him for being so much better than me and for causing me to be obsessed with him. Also he's stupid!

Raymond Anderson says: 18 November 2009, 12:01 am

One of the greatest put downs I ever heard was: 'sorry, that's about as interesting as Charlie Drake's last fart.'

Laxative says: 18 November 2009, 12:23 am

@arse. I though you were supposed to be the bozo with verbal diarrhoea. What's the matter? Do you need an enema or have you finally realised you've made a complete tit of yourself?

Poop Report says: 18 November 2009, 12:27 am

I have the shits big time, I came on this blog and worked my mouth off on the comments and I felt really poorly the following day and I've had the shits ever since. ...

This is not Murray Bookchin says: 18 November 2009, 10:35 am

Have you ever wondered which hurts the most: saying something and wishing you had not, or saying nothing, and wishing you had?

Dr Brooke Magnanti says: 18 November 2009, 1:03 pm

We don't need to be clever to learn your lies. We only have to listen, open up our eyes.

Belle de Jour says: 18 November 2009, 1:28 pm
If Brooke Magnanti isn't Belle de Jour then Michael K must be the Queen of Sheba!

Lisa Hilton says: 18 November 2009, 1:42 pm

No, I'm Belle de Jour and Dave Kelso-Mitchell is the Queen of Sheba!

Frosty the Snowman says: 18 November 2009, 2:05 pm

Aristotle Onassis didn't really die, his death was faked, and he wrote Belle de Jour. Onassis is Mister Big and he's behind everything including the complete works of Shakespeare!

The Queen of Sheba says: 18 November 2009, 2:34 pm

I'll buy that for a dollar.

fi says: 18 November 2009, 2:35 pm

I think I'll become a Christian. I already look like one.

dave kelso-mitchell says: 18 November 2009, 4:12 pm

For any American friends reading this, the word 'arse' is a British word roughly equivalent to the American 'ass' (as in 'asshole').

But you'd probably figured that out from the comments being left.

oldrope says: 18 November 2009, 4:48 pm

Hey, Trip didn't write the blog or the books, but he did spend fourteen months around 2003 having sex for money whilst working as a high-class call girl.

By weird and ironic coincidence he also spent the time between 27 September 2007 to 15 November 2007 pretending to be Billie Piper.

Which is another weird coincidence since Trip doesn't even write this blog, Billie Piper does.

All of which is a weird coincidence since I don't believe in coincidence.

Christopher Nosnibor says: 18 November 2009, 6:57 pm

...and I couldn't possibly comment on the rumours that I in fact wrote much of the work credited to 'Stewart Home' (apart from that penned by Richard Allen, of course).

dave kelso-mitchell says: 18 November 2009, 7:31 pm

Ha—but I've just realised that Nosnibor spelled sideways is 'Nibonosr'.

Sprunggg!

The 'Fake' Lady Black of Crossharbour (Isle of Dogs) says: 18 November 2009, 9:24 pm

Actually I'm Belle de Jour…and I'm also once, twice, three times a lady, even if stuck up toffs think I'm no Lady at all! And just wait until Conrad proves that the Chicago trial was a stitch up, gets out of jail and we sue the arse off every stuck-up fucker who told lies about us and called me an Anglo-Canadian Imelda Marcos… Tossers!

Therese says: 18 November 2009, 10:14 pm

Next you will be trying to tell us you did not write Sarah Palin's book you rich shady crawling little grub…

I Was Paris Hilton's Double says: 18 November 2009, 10:30 pm

…or telling us that airheads are like so last year!

Joseph Kessel says: 18 November 2009, 10:44 pm

And don't forget that the real reason I wrote Belle de Jour is to prove that you can't fool all the people all the time! This appears to be a lesson that Conrad Black has yet to fully learn despite being jailed!

Stephen Hawking says: 18 November 2009, 10:50 pm

Did you know that William Shakespeare is in fact the author of the works of Shakespeare? That said, we do know that others sometimes revised the texts and that Thomas Middleton, in performing such work on *Macbeth*, contributed the witches scene to the Scottish play.

http://en.wikipedia.org/wiki/William_Shakespeare

J. Edgar Hoover says: 18 November 2009, 11:12 pm

I've had my men investigate Stewart Home and I have no doubt that he is both a red and a subversive, not to mention the real author of the Belle de Jour books and blog. Home can do anything but he can't do everything, and since he was born several hundred years after the works attributed to Shakespeare were composed, my men have concluded he did not write *Macbeth* or any of the other plays by the same hand. He is, however, a master of disguise and I was so jealous of his collection of dresses that I had my men steal them. I've destroyed them all trying to get into them since they are way too small for me. So forget Henry, stick with J. Edgar, a Hoover name you can trust! And if you have any spare dresses lying around, don't forget to send them to me at FBI HQ!

That Boy Owen says: 18 November 2009, 11:24 pm

Come, Brooke, come feel my love muscle!

Hugh Grant says: 18 November 2009, 11:46 pm

I wrote Belle de Jour to prove I could have been what I always wanted to be—A WOMAN!

Divine Brown says: 18 November 2009, 11:53 pm

He could have been...could have been...whereas I have been an actor among other things...

Jude Law says: 18 November 2009, 11:56 pm

Actually I wrote the Belle de Jour book and blogs to prove I'm a consummate actor, and I could sustain something like this over 6 years!

Dr Brooke Magnanti presents the National Lottery in Drag says: 19 November 2009, 12:04 am

Belle de Jour—it could be YOU!

Eddie Izzard says: 19 November 2009, 12:06 am

I'm a transvestite, get me out of here!

The Singing Nun says: 19 November 2009, 12:09 am

My dick is so big, it was overthrown by a military coup. It's now known as the Democratic Republic of My Dick.

The Cross-Dressing Ronald Reagan says: 19 November 2009, 12:14 am

Three vampires walk into a bar. One orders a blood on the rocks. Another orders a double blood. The third simply asks for a mug of hot water.

'Why didn't you order blood like everyone else?', asks the bartender.

The vampire pulls out a tampon and says, 'I'm making tea!'

Victor Grayson says: 19 November 2009, 12:19 am

I do not believe that we are divinely destined to be drudges. We must break the rules of the rich and take our destinies into our own hands.

jim seventies says: 19 November 2009, 12:28 am

I didn't read any of the above posts.

Clyde Tolson says: 19 November 2009, 12:31 am
'Stewart Home is my alter ego. He can read my mind.'

fi says: 19 November 2009, 2:27 am

'I think I'll become a Christian. I already look like one.'

I didn't write this.

Leo Tolstoy says: 19 November 2009, 4:23 am

Chumley, why didn't I know sooner? You could have written friggin' *War and Peace* and saved me a lot of time, I coulda been sexting…

fi says: 19 November 2009, 6:25 am

'I think I'll become a Christian. I already look like one.'

I didn't write that.

The Singing Postman says: 19 November 2009, 7:20 am

I'm a high class prostitute but I've had to subsidise my income by working as a research scientist. It's just not possible for a girl to earn enough money at an honest profession any more.

fi says: 19 November 2009, 7:24 am

'I think I'll become a Christian. I already look like one.'

I didn't write that. At least, I think I didn't. It's hard some days to remember exactly who I am…

The totally real Tom McCarthy says: 19 November 2009, 8:05 am

Everyone knows I wrote *Macbeth*; it was even in *Frieze* magazine.

Macbeth says: 19 November 2009, 9:26 am.

What bloody man is that!

Alf Garnett says: 19 November 2009, 9:27 am.

What bloody man is that!

arse says: 19 November 2009, 9:29 am.

I am paranoid that a bird will shit on my head someday and I don't know why…

Alf Garnett says: 19 November 2009, 9:31 am.

If a bird shat on my head I'd slap the dirty cow. You should be more careful about who you're going out with my son!

Charles Atlas says: 19 November 2009, 9:49 am.

I was a ninety-seven pound weakling until I wrote Belle de Jour: *The Intimate Adventures of a London Call Girl* (although actually we call them hookers in The States, and in reality I was being punked out as a rent boy...)

Friends of Lucie Blackman, The Real Belle de Jour says: 19 November 2009, 10:26 am

Turning tricks is my favourite activity. I can't go a day without turning a trick because I need the money to feed my drug habit!

This is not Xaviera Hollander says: 19 November 2009, 10:29 am

But I'm a 'Happy Hooker' and I wrote Belle de Jour...

We are not the Barclay Brothers! says: 19 November 2009, 11:19 am

Whoring may be one way to earn a living, but it is not the best way to become seriously rich. What have we got? A reclusive billionaire life-style in London, Monaco and the Channel Islands. A media portfolio—we own The Telegraph Group, and we'll use it more sensibly than a criminal idiot like Conrad Black! Not to mention all our other business interests—we own the Woolworths name now too, and Littlewoods, both bought from bankruptcy!

Duncan Webb says: 19 November 2009, 11:53 am

Actually Dr Brooke Magnanti didn't write the Belle de Jour book and blogs, isn't it apparent to everyone that only Martin Amis is capable of writing prose that bad and that tedious? However, Magnanti did work as a high-class prostitute when completing her PhD and the list of her clients is a lot more interesting than the 'real' identity of Belle de Jour. I tell you the stuff I've got on Magnanti's men is dynamite—top politicians, clerics, gangsters, spies and enemy diplomats, all at the same time. Once we get this past the newspaper libel lawyers you'll witness the greatest scandal since the Profumo Affair! Heck, she even slept with Jack Spot, Billy Hill, Albert Dimes and me!

The Other Margaret Thatcher says: 19 November 2009, 12:21 pm

Are you all stupid? I wrote Belle de Jour. I needed something to keep me amused after I retired from politics!

Mary Whitehouse says: 19 November 2009, 12:28 pm

Actually I wrote Belle de Jour to expose the evils of prostitution. Have you all forgotten about W. T. Stead and his crusading articles in the *Pall Mall Gazette* entitled *The Maiden Tribute of Modern Babylon*?

http://en.wikipedia.org/wiki/The_Maiden_Tribute_of_Modern
_Babylon

Jilly Johnson says: 19 November 2009, 12:30 pm

They are all lying. I wrote Belle de Jour as a way of making cash once I was too old to work in the front line of the glamour industry!

The Fake Sammy Marshall says: 19 November 2009, 12:32 pm

Actually I wrote Belle de Jour and I'm still working the front end of the glamour industry, as well as moving into the back end!

Tina Small says: 19 November 2009, 12:38 pm

They're all claiming to be Belle de Jour 'cos they've got breast envy, they're all jealous of my eighty-four inch boobs and crave the kind of attention I get!

Hugh Cornball says: 19 November 2009, 12:43 pm.

Got 28-32-84 tits!
Michael K says: 19 November 2009, 12:44 pm

I could have sworn somebody else said that!

Gary Bullshitter says: 19 November 2009, 12:49 pm

Strangled? Leave it out Charlie, it's a geezer wearing make-up! And what I say is earn a ton from off-the-books night work and then when the Giro arrives lie back to enjoy another SE7 dole day! There's no place like Charlton for knocking up the fake memoirs of a tart with a PhD in complete fakery!

Gary's Gang says: 19 November 2009 at 12:55 pm

Keep on dancin'…

Gary Glitter says: 19 November 2009, 12:56 pm

I'm the man who put the bang in gang…

People of the World says: 19 November 2009, 12:57 pm

Rot in hell you stupid nonce!

The (Un)real Henry Kissinger says: 19 November 2009, 1:08 pm

You're all a bunch of asses, or arses as you limey's say, I wrote Belle de Jour. You can kiss my ass. Kissinger by name and kiss and tellin' yer by nature. I survived Tricky Dicky's administration and being on the board for Conrad Black when he went down, so I'm more than capable of faking the confessions of a London call girl!

The ghost on the coast says: 19 November 2009, 1:21 pm
'Dr Brooke Magnanti' is an anagram of 'RTD ER Mangina Book'. A thinly veiled hint that Russell T Davies and the Queen are the true co-authors of the Belle de Jour writings. Obvious when you think about it.

arse says: 19 November 2009, 1:33 pm

Having read through the comments on these pages, any sane person can see that Mobile-Home has all the big hitters covering up for him, from the Barclay Brothers via Margaret Thatcher to Henry Kissinger himself! It must be obvious by now that Mobile-Home is Mister Big! He controls the conspiracy to destroy the world, and is in fact an alien from outer space. Unless Mobile-Home is stopped now it could be the end of life on earth as we know it!

I was Paul Gilroy's Double says: 19 November 2009, 1:48 pm

In fact I wrote Belle de Jour to explore W. E. B. du Bois's notion of double-conciousness:

http://en.wikipedia.org/wiki/Double_consciousness

Valerie Solanas says: 19 November 2009, 2:01 pm

In fact, I wrote the Belle de Jour books and blogs in 1966 as a sci-fi satire of a future society in which capitalism and patriarchy had not been defeated.

Tuesday Kid says: 19 November 2009, 6:15 pm

You're known for your art pranks Home. This could still be a double bluff.

arse says: 19 November 2009, 11:05 pm

Having read through the comments on these pages, any sane person can see that Mobile-Home has all the big hitters covering up for him, from the Barclay Brothers via Margaret Thatcher to Henry Kissinger himself! It must be obvious by now that Mobile-Home is Mister Big! He controls the conspiracy to destroy the world, and is in fact an alien from outer space. Unless Mobile-Home is stopped now it could be the end of life on earth as we know it!

oh—I said that already didnt I?

Le Comte de Saint Germain says: 20 November 2009, 12:38 am

Everybody knows that I am immortal. Over the centuries I have taken on new identities and one of the more recent was Belle de Jour. I used my knowledge gained over many lifetimes to compose the books and blog attributed to Belle. When you think about it, she could only be me! Don't be fooled, Brooke is just my patsy!

Christopher Nosnibor says: 20 November 2009, 10:58 pm

Quoting '*dave kelso-mitchell*, 18 November 2009, 7:31 pm'

'Ha—but I've just realised that Nosnibor spelled sideways is 'Nibonosr'. Sprunggg!'

Damn, you got me, Dave. The fact that my name contains letters that can be used to spell 'bono' is no coincidence, either—every song ever recorded by U2 was in fact written by me also. Unfortunately, I was using Leonard Cohen's accountant and have been forced to start writing books under my own name, and supplementing my income by working as an assassin. I'll come clean: I killed Michael Jackson, and Kanye West is just another of my pseudonyms...

I'm Mandy Fly Me says: 23 November 2009, 11:23 pm

Completely quaaluded.

Howling Wizard, Shrieking Toad says: 24 November 2009, 9:58 am

Rather than being a twenty-nine year old lady of the night, 'Belle de Jour' is in fact the male writer Stewart Home, forty-two, known under his own name for the novels in which he interweaves lurid pornographic descriptions with high-brow literary and cultural criticism...

Very Sunny Meadow says: 25 November 2009, 9:25 am

Did you see what the fools at *Principia Dialectica* wrote on this subject a week ago?

'For years some media pundits and rumour mongers went round claiming to know who was Belle de Jour; some even claimed they were Belle. What do you know...But they do not have her talent, all they can do is worship violence, speak of the fetishism of violence, it makes you sick, especially when that sort of material falls in the hands of vulnerable young people. Many youngsters worship their idols who earn a lot of dosh kicking footballs or rapping the night away. But as work has dwindled many people are left with nothing to do, hence the gangs who roam the streets. Violence comes in all sorts of shapes. It is horrific. One cannot have illusions about lumpen elements. They invariably join a militia when things get worse. History teaches us that it is indeed what took place in Germany (the SA, SS), in France (the Petainist Milice), the list is endless. Maybe Dr Brooke Magnanti will have to get a real critical dialogue instead of doing surface stuff. As for those who claimed to be her, we send them our fraternal greetings. So long suckers!'

Of course since as far as I know no-one (not even Lisa Hilton) actually claimed to be Belle de Jour, you're left wondering who on earth they could mean—unless, that is, you are already familiar with their obsessions. Naturally, I am, and I know how to wind them up and exploit them! Prigent is thus once again left looking like a right charlie!

Doris Stokes says: 25 November 2009, 4:46 pm

You boys are all very silly. I think Stewart and The Real Monty Cantsin should get together for a proper package tour of the United Kingdom just like when Buddy Holly and The Big Bopper did it.

Now I'll have my tea and then iron your uniform.

shit says: 8 December 2009, 9:33 am

What do you mean, 'Belle's' prose is bad? If she were really someone other than you, Home, then that other person has made much more money than you, surely, by churning out some very well-conceived and marketed bits of trash. Sounds right up your street, just more successful.

OK if she really weren't you, you wouldn't have so much chance of starting a feud with this other person than you might dream of having in respect of Salman Rushdie, Martin Amis, John Cage's estate, or others higher up the stink-of-shit literary career ladder than yourself. (I guess you were trying to hook Alice Debord with that stupid howlings film too). Or maybe with 'Belle' that's something you were holding a door open to getting around to, at some point, when you called this constructed person's prose bad.

As for your cheap dig at the marketing of the works as 'authentic', this is just as hypocritical as the rest of your attitude. There are many, many things you've written where you've attempted to portray your own bullshit as authentic, e.g. about the early years of Class War. You knew the 'truth' and everyone else was stupid, right

You're whole self-portrayal is as Mr Authentic the Artist—whatever self-descriptions you might use.

But of course many people really are so stupid as to judge people by self-descriptions. Oh no, Home isn't 'authentic'—he's far too sophisiticated for that. Yeah, right.

Your basic right-wing attitude is that everyone's either in it for the money or too stupid to know that being in it for the money is the only sensible reason for doing anything.

For decades you have presented your cynicism about everything other than your own career as being the only authenticity worth having. Just you haven't used that word, because if you did your pigshit-stupid followers would have nowhere to stand.

I hope you like hospital food.

You're a complete and utter cunt, you know it, and oh look, here are all your little followers and copiers coming along to say what they think might impress you.

Home wrote Wombat 92 says: 8 December 2009, 9:39 am

Michel isn't perfect but he's sincere.

For that reason, whatever he writes is far more useful than Home's complete collected works.

mistertrippy says: 8 December 2009, 10:14 am

Haven't you got anything better to do with your time than make a fool of yourself here? You must be the most boring person in the world. And while I didn't write Wombat 92 or Belle de Jour, the name you've used here ('Home wrote Wombat 92') is evidence of the tedious way you operate. Virtually no one believed the ridiculous lie that I wrote Belle de Jour and now that has finally become evident even to you, we see you switch to another boring lie (which, don't forget, was also included in the original fraudulent document claiming I 'was' Belle de Jour). I'm sure you love being this deluded since it enables you to avoid dealing with the fact you could bore the pants off a corpse that has been lying in a grave for months... A hundred years of sleep has got to be more entertaining than your endless drivel. If you actually got yourself a life you might stand some chance of ceasing to cut such a sorry figure.

Home wrote Wombat 92, Crown Against Concubine, Green and Brown Anarchist, Christ/Marx/Satan, etc., says:
8 December 2009, 11:31 am

For fuck's sake, don't tell us you're opposed to the issuing of 'fraudulent' documents! You prefer them 'authentic', then? You've been issuing fraudulent documents for twenty-five years.

You've done it among:
anarchists, Leninists, neo-Nazis, greens, Satanists, Christians, right-wing conspiracists, pagans, artists, sex workers, cultists, druids.

Of course you wrote Wombat 92.

The Magnanti ploy doesn't get you off the hook. You wrote Belle too, but even if you weren't the author and Very Sunny Meadows got it wrong, don't think you can get away with using that as 'evidence' that you didn't write W92. You can fool all the suckers most of the time, but you can't fool everyone all the time.

Fucking curious that you don't want to admit to W92 nearly twenty years later, even though keeping quiet about it doesn't net you any money, and everyone knows you enjoy winding people up and boasting about it afterwards—with the mentality of the right-wing cunt ex-public schoolboy that you have so clearly got even if you're not one. So why did you write it? Why would you waste your ever-so valuable time, as a terribly interesting person and celebrity, winding up a bunch of soap-averse petty-bourgeois drop-out anarchists not one of whom you often even bumped into socially, unless you had a very clear aim?

Don't think you weren't rumbled years ago. The W92 allegation was deliberately put into the Very Sunny Meadows material in order to get a response.

It was noted that even when you were in the middle of doing your post-modernist shtick to the *Guardian* (did I write Belle or didn't I?), you took care to implicitly deny W92.

However, you didn't bother to deny what we actually did invent that was wholly fictitious, namely the allegation that you wrote a document called *Neither Ra Nor Osiris: Towards the Supersession of Freemasonry*, which didn't even exist. We employed psy-ops, you see. We're not as stupid as you think. How scintillating your pathetic 'media and standing in front of a mirror admiring your haircut before you go to parties' life must be. We met you once; you bored the shit out of us.

mistertrippy says: 8 December 2009, 3:54 pm

Anyone who goes back and checks what I said to the *Guardian* will see you are lying and/or deluded (probably both). You send me to sleep. ZZZZZZZZZZZZZZzzzzzzzzzzzzzzzzzz...

Home wrote Wombat 92 says: 8 December 2009, 5:30 pm

Great—stay asleep—you're not our intended audience here. Didn't Home look a fool, he who's issued fraudulent documents for the last quarter-century?

An Old Hand Who Knows the Ropes says: 8 December 2009, 6:43 pm

You're the one who looks like a fool and an obsessive too. You keep making ridiculous claims and there are paranoids out there who will think you are a cop with all this talk of psy-ops. Are you nuts?

Home wrote Wombat 92 says: 8 December 2009, 7:37 pm

Yeah sure, we're complete nuts. But why would cops want to undermine Home's efforts? And who cares whether someone who's not interested in the content of what we've posted thinks we're cops or not? We certainly don't. They're not our intended audience either. Obsessive, yes, we often are and on many things. Incidentally, dig your language skills—the only sentence that wasn't a double-insulter was your last. Anyway, the hell with you if you're not interested in content, Mr Knows the Ropes. 'If you talk about psy-ops, paranoids will think you're a cop' is the most ridiculous thing we've heard all day. What else shouldn't we talk about? So you know all about psy-ops, right, but are so suss you don't talk about it? What do you talk about? Practical history in the fucking night-clubs?

CNN says: 8 December 2009, 8:36 pm

Having gone to such great lengths to detail who your intended audience isn't, care to share as to precisely who are your intended audience (bearing in mind where you're posting)?

Home wrote the complete works of Shakespeare says: 8 December 2009, 10:53 pm

We can't allow anyone to be as cynical as Home, if we do he will undermine all the moral foundations underpinning capitalist society… and besides he might even trick some dim-wit counter-revolutionaries into extending the comments on one of his blogs to page three! You'd have to be a real idiot to fall for that one, so we won't!

The Polar Bear Who Came in From the Cold says: 8 December 2009, 10:57 pm

PAGE THREE!

Jilly Johnson (Page three) says: 8 December 2009, 11:04 pm

Page three, that's me! But don't forget: 'Home wrote the complete works of Shakespeare'. Keep repeating it and if you're a nutter you'll start believing it, but most people won't just as they don't believe he is Belle de Jour….

Howling Wizard, Shrieking Toad says: 9 December 2009, 2:13 am

Some of the comments here look like they come from the *Principia Dialectica* corner—yawwwwnnnnnn...

howling wizard, shrieking toad says: 9 December 2009, 5:56 am

The Home 'critics' here seem to think they have all rights to how Debord et al are understood and perceived by 'history', and that everyone else who has their take on it is somehow a 'phony' or a lackey or a fake of some kind. But it's boring. And their (apparent) stagnation, ossification and deification of people like Postone is boring too. And no, I am not a 'Stewart Home groupie' as you characterise those who like his books.

Home seems to have a far sharper, funnier, more interesting take on the absurdity and redundancy of all right-wing schools of thought and left-wing schools of thought than many—that clearly annoys you. He can also see, like many of us, how the two 'extremes' end up being as vacuous, sinister and banal as each other.

Home Tricked Wombat 92 into taking us to page three says: 9 December 2009, 7:54 am

And don't forget that Home wrote the *Complete Works Of Shakespeare* in the evening, when he was taking time out from being Sir Francis Bacon and writing up the experiments that become the foundational works of modern science. And, of course, Home also wrote the *Oxford English Dictionary*.

Home wrote the Oxford English Dictionary says: 9 December 2009, 8:39 am

Now Wombat 92 has been told the score, they'd have to be a real idiot to take it to page four; Wombat is a nutter but are they enough of a nutter to do just that?

But page three, PAGE THREE, it's the place for me!

Howling Wizard, Shrieking Toad says: 9 December 2009, 9:56 am

Well, speaking plainly now, the image of a frozen reality that nevertheless is caught up in an unremitting, ghostly movement at once becomes meaningful when this reality is dissolved into the process of which man is the driving force—That can be seen only from the standpoint of one who sees the complete breakdown of any semblance of what we understood, and perceived the left/right dialectic to be, because the meaning of these tendencies is now laid naked within the 'phantomic' presence of globalization in the early twenty-first century.

Principia Dialectica and Postone, in their 'unremitting seriousness' fail to comprehend that.[3]

3. The comments on Home's Mister Trippy blog are laid out at 50 per page. Wombat 92 left the 101th comment, taking this material to page 3. Although the blog in its recent run was hosted at http://stewarthomesociety.org/blog, Home posted the first season of his Mister Trippy series on MySpace, where there was often euphoria in the comments every time they transferred to a new page (the comments on Home's daily MySpace blog often ran to 10 pages, or around 500 replies).

Index of Abandoned Material

27. Sharon Lockhart Likes to be Taken Hard and Penetrated Deeply!

28. King-Size Cock for David Hockney!

29. See Claude Cahun Experience Incredible, Powerful Orgasms as you Enter Her!

30. Helen Chadwick is Wet and Horny! Don't Disappoint Her! Get a Bigger Cock Today!

31. Blow Faith Wilding Away with your Enlarged Prick!

32. Click Here to Find Out What Barbara Hepworth REALLY Wants!

33. Make Jenny Holzer's Mind Up for her by Adding Three INCHES To Your Cock!

34. Watch Abigail Lane Come Again & Again. Make Your Dick Two Inches Bigger!

35. Nancy Spero Loves Being Penetrated Deeply and Fully by your Huge Schlong!

36. Pleasure Elizabeth Wright Like Never Before with a Larger Lovestick!

37. Ever Heard the Sound of a Huge One Slapping Against June Wayne's Tight Butt?

38. Ram Your Bigger and Better Gun Into Gilbert & George and Hear Them Moan!

39. Give Cornelia Parker a Mind Blowing Orgasm!

40. Impress Mary Kelly! Your Bulge Never Felt So Big!

41. Give Zoe Smith More Pleasure in Bed by Adding Girth and Length!

42. Seven Inches is Simply Not Big Enough to Pleasure the Guerrilla Girls!

43. If you Can't Make Emma Kay Come, you Need a Larger Schlong for Sure!

44. Let Christine Borland Choose Between a Rock and a Hard DlCK!

45. Give Leonora Carrington a Ride on your ROCKET!

46. Boost your Chances With Barbara Kruger by Enlarging your Instrument!

47. Your Throbbing Missile is Ready to Fire into Gillian Wearing!

48. Show Angela Bulloch you're the Dog's Bollocks with a Nine Inch Cock!

48. Bridget Riley Can't Stand It! She'll Play with your Donger All Night Long!

49. Milly Thompson Loves Men with Thick, Muscular Cocks that Keep on all Night Long!

50. Give Tina Keane a Beautiful Present! Buy our Penis Enlargement Pills!

51. Suzanne Lacy Loves Men with Huge Cocks and Spades of Confidence!

52. Your Enlarged Package will Satisfy Pamela Rosenkranz no End!

53. Let Ida Kar Experience a New you; Get your Huge New Dick Here!

54. Leave Lubaina Himid Speechless with your Legendary New Cock!

55. Amaze Louise Lawler by Turning your Garden Tool into a POWER DRILL!

56. Girth and Growth Go Hand in Hand with Giving Vanessa Beecroft Hours of Fun!

57. Jacqueline de Jong Loves Men with Huge Equipment—Do you Measure Up?

58. Sophie Calle Wants you to be a Stud In Bed—Unleash your Potential!

59. Your Hot Rod will Heat Up Katharina Fritsch's Bedroom!

60. Angelina Gualdoni Loves a Huge Dick, Get One Here!

61. Grayson Perry Dresses as a College Cheerleader & Fucks For Cash!!!

62. Stewart Home wants to Deep Throat your New HUGE Dick![4]

4. Note the above listed chapters were all completed and comprised a part of the first draft of this book. The 'author' abandoned them during the novel's redrafting and prior to it entering any form of collaborative editing process. These abandoned sections have not in any way been censored or suppressed. They were simply dropped in order to improve the overall structure of this work and provide the best possible reading experience.

Blood Rites of the Bourgeoisie
Stewart Home
Semina No. 7
Published and distributed by Book Works, London

ISBN 978 1 906012 23 6

Commissioning editor: Stewart Home
Edited by Mister Trippy and Gavin Everall
Proofread by Eileen Daly
Designed by Fraser Muggeridge studio
Printed by Die Keure, Bruges

Book Works
19 Holywell Row
London
EC2A 4JB
www.bookworks.org.uk
tel: +44 (0)20 7247 2203

Book Works is funded by Arts Council England